Lin

BOUNTY HUNTERS

Bounty
Hunters

LEFT BEHIND

>THE KIDS<

Jerry B. Jenkins

Tim LaHaye

WITH CHRIS FABRY

TYNDALE HOUSE PUBLISHERS, INC.
WHEATON, ILLINOIS

Visit Tyndale's exciting Web site at www.tyndale.com

Discover the latest Left Behind news at www.leftbehind.com

Published in association with the literary agency of Alive Communications, Inc., 7680 Goddard Street, Suite 200, Colorado Springs, CO 80920.

Edited by Lorie Popp

ISBN 0-8423-5804-8, mass paper

Printed in the United States of America

08 07 06 05 04

8   7   6   5   4   3   2

To the memory of
Col. Charles R. Smith, USMC, Ret.

TABLE OF CONTENTS

THE YOUNG TRIBULATION FORCE

Original members—Vicki Byrne, Judd Thompson, Lionel Washington

Other members—Mark, Conrad, Darrion, Janie, Charlie, Shelly, Melinda

OTHER BELIEVERS

Chang Wong—Chinese teenager working in New Babylon

Westin Jakes—pilot for singer Z-Van

Tsion Ben-Judah—Jewish scholar who writes about prophecy

Colin and Becky Dial—Wisconsin couple with an underground hideout

Sam Goldberg—Jewish teenager, Lionel's good friend

Mr. Mitchell Stein—Jewish friend of the Young Trib Force

Naomi Tiberius—computer whiz living in Petra

Chaim Rosenzweig—famous Israeli scientist

Tanya Spivey—daughter of Mountain Militia leader, Cyrus Spivey

Cheryl Tifanne—pregnant young lady from Iowa

Zeke Zuckermandel—disguise specialist for the Tribulation Force

Marshall Jameson—leader of the Avery, Wisconsin believers

UNBELIEVERS

Nicolae Carpathia—leader of the Global Community

Leon Fortunato—Carpathia's right-hand man

Z-Van—lead singer for the popular group The Four Horsemen

What's Gone On Before

JUDD Thompson Jr. and the rest of the Young Tribulation Force are living the adventure of a lifetime. After a narrow escape from the Global Community in Jerusalem, Judd and Lionel try to rescue their friend Westin Jakes from an evil plan. In the process, Perryn Madeleine, a young man from France, loses his life.

Vicki Byrne, held captive by a group of Mountain Militia followers, reaches out to Tanya Spivey. When Tanya becomes a true believer, her father gets angry and threatens Vicki.

In Petra, Sam Goldberg witnesses the most incredible miracle he has ever seen as Nicolae Carpathia drops bombs on the red rock city. Sam begins to tell others around the world what has happened in his e-mails titled the Petra Diaries.

Judd keeps in contact with Chang Wong in New Babylon to see if the Tribulation Force can give Judd and Lionel a flight home. Instead, Judd is given the chance to stay in France and fulfill the vision of a young man he never met.

When Mark gets angry at Vicki for putting the group in danger, Vicki's world changes and she volunteers to leave.

Join the Young Tribulation Force as they make important decisions in the most terrifying time in world history.

ONE

Message of Mercy

JUDD Thompson Jr. stared at Jacques Madeleine in disbelief. Judd had known this man less than twenty-four hours, but he already felt like the father Judd no longer had.

Jacques' son, Perryn, had been killed by Z-Van the night before. Now Jacques was asking Judd to stay in France and finish his son's dream: to turn the chateau into an international ministry station.

"With your contacts in the States and around the world, you could be an asset to our group," Jacques said. "We could reach many."

Judd started to speak, but Jacques closed his eyes and shook his head. "Please, think about this. Pray. Talk with your friends." He put an arm around Judd. "Lionel mentioned there is someone special waiting for you."

Judd nodded, and for the first time felt he could share his feelings about Vicki with someone older. He told Jacques everything, from their first meeting and all the catastrophes they had survived, to their many disagreements.

The man listened intently, asking questions and smiling as Judd told his story. Jacques asked if Judd had a picture of Vicki, and Judd opened his wallet. A friend had taken a snapshot a few years earlier while Judd and Vicki edited the *Underground* newspaper. Judd had been upset with Ryan Daley for taking the picture, but now it was one of his prized possessions.

In the picture, Vicki stood by Judd, her red hair touching the desktop. As Ryan had snapped the photograph, Vicki glanced at the camera, showing the trace of a smile.

"I can see why you would want to get back," Jacques said. "She is beautiful."

"I'm worried about the way we fought. I was a real jerk."

Jacques lifted his eyebrows. "We are all jerks in one way or another. If she has said she is willing to forgive you, she must have feelings for you."

"Did you and your wife fight before you were married?"

Jacques patted Judd's shoulder. "When two

people come together, no matter how like-minded they are, you must expect friction. That process knocks many of the rough edges off both people."

Judd pursed his lips. He knew there were more rough edges to him than he wanted to admit. But Vicki had some too.

"It might be easier and safer to get your friend here than you going back there," Jacques said. "Or we could arrange for all of your friends to join us."

Judd put a hand on the man's shoulder. "Your son had a great vision for this place. I think God's going to use it, but I'm not sure if I'm supposed to be involved."

Vicki Byrne had seen leaving her friends as her only alternative. Mark had stated clearly that either she left or he would.

Colin and Becky Dial immediately asked Vicki to reconsider. Shelly said she would leave too if Mark forced Vicki to go. Conrad and Mark kept quiet, and Tanya Spivey, the newest person to join them at the Wisconsin safe house, was speechless.

"If I stay, I'll just mess things up," Vicki said. "It's better this way."

"How have you messed things up?" Tanya

said. "If you hadn't found me, I wouldn't be a believer."

Conrad sat forward, his elbows on his knees, and glanced at Mark. "Vicki understands she made mistakes. Sending her away right now will only put her in more danger."

"I'm not trying to endanger her," Mark said. "I think there should be a consequence for her actions, even if she just wanted to help somebody. This isn't the first time this has happened."

"I'm glad she took the chance," Tanya said.

"Maybe I'll take Tanya with me," Vicki suggested.

"I assume you've prayed about this," Colin said.

Vicki cringed. Yes, she had prayed about it. She'd done nothing but pray, and God still seemed distant and silent. Her decision to leave came as much from frustration as it did from believing it was the best thing to do.

"Is there anybody else you can talk to about this?" Becky said. "Anybody you trust?"

Vicki thought of several people she would like to talk with. Judd. Ryan. Bruce. Two of them were dead, and Judd was halfway around the world. A face flashed in her mind, and she turned to Becky. "Chloe

Williams. She really seemed interested in me when we talked a long time ago."

"Write her," Colin said. "And we'll trust you to come to a good decision."

Sam Goldberg stood engrossed by the scene in Petra. Hundreds of thousands turned their attention to Tsion Ben-Judah as he stood high above the crowd. He seemed embarrassed by the people's cheers. When they finally quieted, Tsion asked that they silently thank God for his love and mercy the next time he was introduced.

Sam had waited for this moment since arriving at Petra. Millions around the globe had learned from this man through his daily writings, and now Sam stood in his presence.

"In the fourteenth chapter of the Gospel of John, our Lord, Jesus the Messiah, makes a promise we can take to the bank of eternity," Tsion began. "He says, 'Let not your heart be troubled; you believe in God, believe also in me. In my father's house are many mansions; if it were not so, I would have told you. I go to prepare a place for you. And if I go and prepare a place for you, I will come again and receive you to myself; that where I am, there you may be also.'

"Notice the urgency. That was Jesus' guarantee that though he was leaving his disciples, one day he would return. The world had not seen the last of Jesus the Christ, and as many of you know, it still has not seen the last of him."

Sam glanced at the computer building and wondered if anyone was recording Tsion's words. He raced to find his friend Naomi Tiberius. This message would be perfect for his next installment of the Petra Diaries.

Chang Wong's heart fluttered as he walked out of Aurelio Figueroa's office. What he had just heard from his boss sickened and petrified him. Chang had often wondered how long he would be able to stay in New Babylon without being discovered, especially with all the tricks he was pulling with secret recordings. Now he would have to be even more careful because the GC were hot on his trail.

When Mr. Figueroa had mentioned Chicago, Chang was even more interested. The Tribulation Force was there, and if Figueroa was right, they were in danger.

Chang had coughed and acted sick in front of his boss until the man ordered him to leave work early. He gathered his things from his desk and quickly walked to the elevators. The GC planned to drop a nuclear bomb on Chicago, and Chang had to warn his friends.

Sam was glad Naomi was recording Tsion's message. He sat outside the building taking notes on a small laptop, listening to Tsion's clear voice hundreds of yards away. God had performed many miracles since Sam's arrival at Petra, and amplifying Tsion's voice seemed a small thing compared to them.

When Tsion finished, Sam went back through his notes and chose highlights. A team of workers inside the computer building had already transcribed Tsion's message, so Sam loaded the document into his computer and began.

Though Sam didn't think of himself as a writer, he knew there were kids around the world who would want to know what was going on in Petra. His first diary account had been well received on theunderground-online.com. Hundreds of e-mails poured in with everything from simple thank-you notes to questions about what catastrophe would come next on God's timetable.

People were still celebrating God's deliverance when Dr. Ben-Judah stood and spoke to us. Following is what he said in my own words. Dr. Ben-Judah asked us to think about the five most important events of history. See if you agree with him.

The first event was God's creation of the world. Second came the worldwide flood of Noah's day. Third, the birth of Jesus Christ.

It was the coming of Jesus that gave us the opportunity to be forgiven by God. Jesus lived a perfect life and died for our sin. Anyone who calls upon him will be saved.

But the story does not end there because, as he predicted, he returned for his true followers three and a half years ago. The Rapture was the fourth pivotal event in history. And the fifth will be his coming one final time.

I have to tell you, this next section of Tsion's message amazed me. Messiah will set up paradise on earth, for he will be in control. This thousand-year period will begin in less than three and a half years, and many believe that since there will be no wars, the population will grow to greater than the number of all the people who have already lived and died up to now.

There will be true peace. No one will starve. Everyone will have enough. We will have this kind of world because God is gracious and good and patient and kind.

Now, an important question: What is your view of God? Where do you get it? The Bible is clear that he is not only all-powerful and all-knowing, but he is also for us, not against us. He is a loving Father who wants to bless our lives. The key to the door of blessing is to give your life to him and ask him to do with it as he will.

We are living in the worst period of human history. Sixteen of the judgments promised in the Bible have struck the earth. There are five more to go before the end of the Great Tribulation.

So how can this God of judgment be called loving? Remember that during this time he is working in people to get them to make a decision. He wants people to call on the name of the Lord.

There are some who will say God is being exclusive. But we must understand that the Bible clearly says that God's will is for all people to be saved. Second Peter 3:9 says, "The Lord is not slack concerning his promise . . . but is long-suffering toward us, not willing that any should perish but that all should come to repentance."

God promised in Joel 2 that he would

"show wonders in the heavens and in the earth: blood and fire and pillars of smoke. The sun shall be turned into darkness, and the moon into blood, before the coming of the great and awesome day of the Lord. And it shall come to pass that whoever calls on the name of the Lord shall be saved. For in Mount Zion and in Jerusalem there shall be deliverance, as the Lord has said, among the remnant whom the Lord calls."

Here I will quote Dr. Ben-Judah word for word as he spoke to the people in Petra.

"Dear people, you are that remnant! Do you see what God is saying? He is still calling men to faith in Christ. He has raised up 144,000 evangelists, from the twelve tribes, to plead with men and women all over the world to decide for Christ. Who but a loving, gracious, merciful, long-suffering God could plan in advance that during this time of chaos he would send so many out in power to preach his message?"

Dr. Ben-Judah reminded us of Eli and Moishe, the two witnesses who preached God's Word at the Wailing Wall. God sent them so people would turn from the lies of the evil one to the truth. All of these things point to the fact that we must make a decision whether to obey the one who rules this world or call upon the name of the Lord.

Dr. Ben-Judah said many will rebel, even some here in Petra, and will choose against this loving God. Don't let this be you. Worship Jesus Christ and turn your life over to him. Receive him right now as the Lamb who will take away your sin. Obey him.

Today something wonderful happened at the end of Tsion's message. I will print his exact words below.

"Messiah was born in human flesh. He came again. And he is coming one more time. I want you to be ready. We were left behind at the Rapture. Let us be ready for the Glorious Appearing. The Holy Spirit of God is moving all over the world. Jesus is building his church during this darkest period in history because he is gracious, loving, long-suffering, and merciful.

"The time is short and salvation is a personal decision. Admit to God that you are a sinner. Acknowledge that you cannot save yourself. Throw yourself on the mercy of God and receive the gift of his Son, who died on the cross for your sin. Receive him and thank him for the gift of your salvation."

When Tsion finished, people bowed their heads and prayed for friends in Petra, for family members and loved ones around the *world. I'm sure some prayed for themselves, accepting the gift God offered to them and the gift he offers you right now. Do not turn away from this. If you are reading my Petra Diaries right now, God is calling you. Pray that prayer with Tsion, and I assure you, if you pray it from your heart and mean it, God will accept you and you will spend eternity with him.*

Vicki rushed to the computer room. It was still early in the morning when Shelly told her she had received a message from Buck Williams. Vicki had quickly written Chloe to see if she could talk about a problem.

> *Vicki,*
>
> *Chloe mentioned you not long ago, and we both prayed for you. She just got back from an amazing trip and is sleeping. I'll have her write you, or if there's a secure phone where you are, she can call.*
>
> *Buck*

Vicki smiled and typed a quick message back. She couldn't wait to talk with Chloe and hear about her trip and how her son,

Kenny, was doing. After sending the message, she clicked the main computer screen. Alarms rang and people came running. Cameras outside the house showed the trees bordering the property and Vicki gasped. Several people from the cave were walking toward Colin's house.

Two

Rescue

Vicki alerted the others about the intruders, and the group moved into action. Colin ordered everyone to stay hidden as he raced upstairs and locked the basement door behind him. Mark focused the cameras, and Vicki counted four people.

"It's my dad and three of his most loyal people," Tanya said.

"You think your father hurt any of the others?" Conrad said.

"Until today I would have said no, but after what he threatened to do to Vicki, I don't know." Tanya turned to Vicki. "I have to go out there. They need to know the truth."

"They wouldn't listen," Vicki said. "The people I'm worried about are the ones that wanted to hear more."

"Yeah, what's he done with Ty?"

"Probably locked up in the back room."

"What are you talking about?" Mark said.

Vicki explained that the group had locked her in a back room and that she had tried to dig her way out through the ceiling. A cave-in had stopped her but left a gaping hole. "I know you're going to think I'm crazy, but we could go back there and get those people while Cyrus is here."

"They'll shoot us," Mark said.

"Not if we crawl through the opening I made." Vicki edged closer and put a hand on Mark's arm. "Please. This is the last thing I'll ever ask. Some of those people wanted to hear more. I think they were ready to pray, but Tanya's father threatened them and came at me with a gun."

Mark looked at the others.

Becky stood and put her hands on her hips. "Colin and I can keep those four busy for a few minutes."

"We'd have to go out the front and circle around so they wouldn't hear us," Conrad said.

"Wait, we don't even know people are being held," Mark said. "They could have run away, or this Cyrus could have convinced them that you and Tanya are nuts."

"I know my brother was interested in

hearing more," Tanya said. "And if I know my dad, he's locked them up until they come to their senses. Now's the time to act."

Conrad took a long breath. "We've always said if there was a chance to reach out and help people become believers, we'd face any danger. Maybe we ought to try."

Shelly stood. "We should go."

Mark threw up his hands and turned to Becky. "Tell Colin what's up. Try to keep those four occupied as long as you can." He looked at Conrad. "Grab the radios. Vicki, get some rope from the storage area. I'll get the night-vision goggles. Let's go."

While Westin watched the latest from the Global Community News Network, Judd took Lionel outside. It took a few moments for Judd to get up the courage to tell Lionel what Jacques had asked.

Lionel's eyes widened as Judd talked. "Are you serious? Stay here?"

"I'm not saying I want to, but maybe God wants us to."

Lionel closed his eyes. "We need to have a serious talk about what God wants and doesn't want. I mean, you're all gung ho to get back to the States, and now you're talking about staying in France?"

"Perryn's death has really affected me. Don't we owe his dad something?"

"Perryn didn't die for us. He died because he believed in God. We owe Jacques our lives, but that doesn't mean we should stay here."

Judd ran a hand through his hair. "I guess I don't know what following God means anymore. We've just spent so much time in Israel, and what did we accomplish?"

"I don't know everything, but God is working. And I believe he's using us, even if we don't understand everything he's doing."

"But what about Z-Van?" Judd said. "If we hadn't rescued him from the earthquake he wouldn't have become such a rabid Carpathia follower. And Perryn would still be alive."

"Maybe. But Westin probably wouldn't be a believer."

"Okay, so why did God put us here with these people?" Judd said, pointing to the chateau.

"To keep us alive, for one thing." Lionel turned and looked at the rippling waters of the pond. "This is a nice place. The people are great. But this is not where I want to be long-term. In three years when Jesus comes back, I'd love to be with my friends and watch the whole thing happen. If I die before then, so be it. If this is where God wants you, stay. I'm headed home as soon as Chang or Westin can work out the details."

"What if we bring everybody here?"

"Think about it. Things are just as hairy there as here. Which is easier, getting three people back there or getting a dozen or more over here?"

"What do you think Westin would say?"

"He's ready now. Says he wants to get involved with the Tribulation Force's Co-op and fly supplies and people all over the world."

Judd sat and put his head in his hands. Why was he feeling such conflict? He ached to see his friends back home, especially Vicki. When Lionel went inside, Judd pulled his wallet from his back pocket and looked at his picture of Vicki.

Vicki and the others hurried along a path at the back of the house. Mark had asked Tanya to stay behind, but she wouldn't hear of it. "I can show you the easiest way to the top of the rocks."

Past the trees, Vicki turned and caught a

glimpse of the four men standing around the back porch, guns cradled in front of them. Mark led the way, working toward the cave at an angle. Tanya rushed forward and pointed them to the right, along a creek.

Vicki clicked her radio twice, the signal that she wanted to talk with Becky.

The woman answered, whispering that the four men had banged on the back door, but Colin hadn't responded. "How close are you?"

"Another ten or fifteen minutes," Vicki said. "What does Colin think of our plan?"

"He's not thrilled, but we'll keep these four as busy as—" Becky clicked off, then returned a few seconds later. "The men are headed back into the woods."

"You have to stop them!"

Becky keyed the microphone as Colin yelled in the background. Becky paused. "Okay, they're turning now. They're coming back. I'll let you know what happens."

Mark and Conrad picked up their pace and told everyone to keep quiet as they neared the cave. Vicki glanced at the jagged rocks of a ravine below and cringed. She had come close to falling into that when she was fumbling in the dark looking for the cave.

Vicki assumed the entrance was being watched, so they skirted the front and followed Tanya to the back. She pointed out a series of footholds the Mountain Militia had used to climb the rocks.

Vicki carried a heavy rope and struggled to keep her balance on the steep incline. She was halfway up when the radio squawked. "I need your help here, Vicki," Becky called.

Everyone stopped and crouched low, hoping those inside the cave hadn't heard the noise. Vicki turned the volume down and clicked her radio.

"The leader of the group wants to talk with Tanya," Becky said. "We've told him she's not here, but he won't believe us."

"Throw a radio out to him," Vicki whispered, taking the rope from her shoulder and tossing it to Mark. She motioned for Tanya to follow, and they moved a few yards into the woods. Vicki explained what had happened and handed Tanya the radio.

Gasping for air, Tanya pressed the talk button and said, "Dad, are you there?"

The sound of Cyrus's voice on the radio sent a chill down Vicki's spine. "Tanya, I want you to walk out of that house right now and come back where you belong."

Mark couldn't find the hole Vicki had told them about on top of the rocks. He noticed a clump of pine trees in a flat area but moved around them. Shelly snapped her fingers and motioned. A crude vent stuck a few inches out of the ground. Beside the vent was a pile of leaves and brush. Mark and Conrad cleared it away and found a dark, plastic covering. Underneath Mark found a hastily constructed ceiling made of wooden boards.

Mark threw off his night-vision goggles and pulled a flashlight from his hip pocket. The beam shone through spaces in the boards, and dust swirled below. Two eyes stared up at him through the darkness. A young man struggled on the ground, gray tape covering his mouth.

"Help me get these boards away from the top," Mark whispered to Shelly and Conrad.

Vicki prayed that Tanya would be able to stall her father. Cyrus's voice seemed to paralyze the girl for a moment, but she caught her breath and pressed the talk button again. "Dad, these people care about me. I don't want to go back with you."

"If you don't come out of there right now, we'll come in and get you."

"Why are you getting so violent?"

"We live by rules, and when those rules are broken, there has to be punishment."

Tanya dipped her head, speechless.

Vicki nudged her. "Talk about your mom."

Tanya nodded. "I've got a question about Mom."

The radio was silent. When Cyrus spoke, his voice sounded different. "Come out here and I'll talk about her."

"You two fought about some things before the disappearances. Did it have anything to do with something new she believed?"

A long pause. "Tanya, let's not go into this now."

"I need to know."

Another pause. Finally Cyrus came back on, his voice thick and stammering. "I . . . uh . . . she said some things that I can't go into, but I assure you, your mother loved you."

"Did she talk about Jesus coming back?" Tanya said. "Did she say anything about your views on God being wrong?"

"We had our differences. She did think I was wrong about a few things, but that didn't mean we didn't love each other."

"Did she ask to talk to Ty and me about it?"

Silence. Tanya gave Vicki a pained look and pushed the button again. "Dad, did

Mom want to tell Ty and me about what she believed?"

"She wasn't thinking clearly. A lot of it didn't make sense. I didn't want her to talk to you until . . . you know . . . until she got things straight in her mind."

"She wanted to tell us the truth, and you wouldn't let her. She wanted to tell us how to follow God, and you made her keep quiet."

Crickets chirped, and Vicki glanced at the top of the rocks. She couldn't tell how Mark and the others were doing. Tanya held the radio by her face, grimacing with each sentence from her father.

"I told her not to talk to you but to write a letter," Cyrus finally said. "She did, and just a couple of days after that she disappeared."

Mark found seven people in the room with duct tape covering their mouths, wrists, and ankles. He cut the young man loose and realized it was Tanya's brother, Ty.

They worked to free the others as Ty whispered his story. "Dad got the gun and asked how many wanted to hear more from Vicki. Everybody who raised a hand got put in here." Ty ripped the tape from a thin woman's mouth.

"Where's Prophet Cy now?" the woman said.

"At the safe house," Mark said. "We have to get you out of here before he comes back."

One by one the captives climbed the rope and into the night air. Conrad and Shelly helped pull each up until they were all outside.

Vicki saw the pain on Tanya's face and wanted to comfort her, but Tanya clutched the radio in a death grip. "Where's the letter?"

"Come out and I'll show you," Cyrus said.

"Tell me where it is, Dad."

"It's at the hideout in my things. I hoped to show it to you one day when you could handle it."

"Have you read it?"

"Yeah. Doesn't make much sense. Just a string of verses and some gibberish she copied from the radio. I do think God will accept her, even if she wasn't thinking clearly."

Tanya handed the radio to Vicki and ran toward the rocks.

"Where are you going?" Vicki called after her.

"I have to find that letter!"

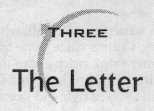

THREE

The Letter

VICKI rushed after Tanya, the radio squawking in her hand. Tanya headed for the rocky area as Vicki pleaded, but the girl kept going through the trees and underbrush. A few people gingerly made their way down the rocks as Tanya started up, and Vicki realized the rescue had been successful.

"If you're not going to talk to me, we're coming in after you," Cyrus said over the radio.

Vicki was glad the radio ruse had kept Cyrus away from the cave, but what about Colin and Becky? Vicki keyed the microphone as she ran. "Mr. Spivey, Tanya's safe. We won't tell anybody about your hiding place."

Cyrus's words were even and slow. "This is your last chance. I don't want anybody hurt, but I'm not leaving here without my daughter."

As Vicki started up the wall, wondering what to say, Colin's voice came over the radio. "Better think twice about that. This place is wired for intruders. One flick of the switch while you're trying to get in and you'll have quite a shock."

"Yeah, right," Cyrus said.

Mark approached Vicki, climbing down the rock. "Where are you going? Everybody's out."

"It's Tanya. There's something inside the cave from her mom."

Mark shook his head and started back up the hill. "We have to stop her before she gets us all killed." He told Conrad and Shelly to move the people away from the cave and head for Colin's house. The group started off in the darkness.

"Does Colin have his house wired for intruders?" Vicki whispered to Mark.

"Not sure. I saw a weird electrical box near the basement though."

The radio filled with static and a strange buzz. When it stopped, Vicki pushed the button. "Mr. Spivey?"

No answer.

Vicki crawled to the top as Mark peered into the room below. She couldn't believe how close she had come to killing herself trying to get out of that hole the night before.

"She's down there with the door open," Mark said. "I'll get her and—"

"No, I know the place. Let me go."

Mark nodded and helped steady the rope as Vicki climbed into the darkened room. She covered a flashlight with her hand and crept through the hall. Voices came from the front of the cave, and Vicki wondered if Tanya had been discovered. She heard rustling in one of the tunnels to her left and found Tanya going through her father's clothes.

"We have to get out of here," Vicki whispered.

"Not until I find it."

"It may be a trick. He knew something about your mom might draw you out."

Tanya threw a garbage bag of clothes in the corner and started on another pile. Something crackled, and Tanya held up a crumpled envelope. "It's got Ty's name and mine on the front." She held the letter to her chest and closed her eyes.

"We don't have time to read it," Vicki said. "Let's get out of here."

They hurried through the kitchen to the back room. Mark was waiting, his head poking through the hole in the ceiling.

When they were outside, the radio

squawked again. "Perimeter two, this is perimeter one," Becky said.

"What's that mean?" Tanya said.

Mark grabbed the radio. "Perimeter two here, go ahead."

"Our bogeys are leaving. Headed home. Be advised."

"Roger. Out."

Mark turned and shoved the radio into his pocket. "Let's go. Tanya's dad and his people are headed this way."

Judd called Chang Wong and reached him in his apartment. Chang seemed glad to talk and told Judd the latest.

"The Tribulation Force's hiding place in Chicago is done," Chang said. "They're going to nuke the city."

"I thought Chicago had already been nuked," Judd said.

"You and everybody else. We planted information that radiation was coming from downtown. It kept everyone safe. Now it's time to move, and I'm having a tough time figuring out where to put all those people."

"It makes my problems seem small." Judd told Chang that Jacques had asked him to stay but that Westin and Lionel wanted to leave.

"It's your call. We don't have any Co-op flights landing near Paris in the next few days. Sounds like we could use Westin if he's a pilot. I'll get back to you on that."

"Where do you think you'll send the Trib Force?"

"I'm waiting for a call about that now. I have places all over, but none big enough to take them all."

Judd mentioned the safe house in Wisconsin as a possibility, and Chang took the information.

When he hung up, Judd stood and looked out the window. Jacques and his wife walked arm in arm near the flower garden their son had planted. The peacefulness of the scene, compared with the death and mayhem going on around the world, nearly overwhelmed him. These two had watched their only son give his life for the cause of Jesus Christ. Was God calling Judd to stay?

It took Vicki several minutes to climb down the rock and join the others. Shouts echoed behind them as they ran through the night. So far, none of the seven new friends had the mark of the believer, but Vicki wanted to talk with them when they reached Colin's house.

Mark held up a hand at the front of the group, so everyone stopped. Vicki turned on her night-vision goggles and saw four figures moving through the trees. When they passed, Mark waved everyone forward.

The reunion at Colin's house almost made Vicki forget about her decision to leave the group. Colin herded everyone downstairs and locked the door. "Cyrus and the other three tried to come in, but they turned back when I activated the electric security system."

"Did you shock them?" Tanya said.

"There are different levels of security. They only got enough power to turn them around."

"Why did they tape you guys up?" Vicki said to Ty.

Ty told them the details of what had happened. "I guess my dad felt it was the only way to keep us in the cave."

"Things are falling apart for Prophet Cy," a bearded man said. "I've seen him get mad. He doesn't give up easy when he has an idea. And if he wants Tanya and Ty back, you can bet he'll come again."

"He can't touch us down here," Vicki said.

While Becky and Colin went for food and Mark and Conrad kept watch on the surveillance cameras, Vicki asked the new people to sit. The group seemed mesmerized by the computer equipment and TV hookup.

Vicki turned on GCNN, and a reporter in New Babylon stood in what looked like an empty parking lot. "It was near this spot that one of the greatest, if not *the* greatest event in world history occurred," the reporter said. "The incredible resurrection of Potentate Nicolae Carpathia. Now filmmaker Lars Rahlmost is almost ready to release his documentary titled *From Death to Life.*"

Rahlmost was shown sitting in a large leather chair, his legs crossed and smoking a pipe. "We've tried to capture the essence of not only Nicolae's rise, but the effect this event had on his followers and even those who are still against him."

Video footage shot with a new type of camera lit up the screen. A close-up of Nicolae's face showed the stone-cold look of a murdered man. But the next moment his eyes fluttered, and soon he sat up in his coffin.

The group from the cave gasped. It was the first time they had heard of Nicolae's resurrection, let alone seen vibrant footage of the event. The report showed clips from interviews with devoted Carpathia followers, people unsure of who the man really was, and even a follower of Jesus in Jerusalem. Rahlmost smirked when he revealed they had lured the follower of Christ into a room by promising him that his message would be broadcast around the world.

The believer was balding and appeared to be middle-aged. He held up a picture of his family, a wife and two young sons, who had disappeared three and a half years earlier. "I can't wait to see them again."

Rahlmost asked questions off camera, and the man spoke of his belief that Carpathia was actually anti-God and perfectly fit the description of the man the Bible labeled the Antichrist.

Rahlmost showed the end of the interview as Global Community officers burst into the room and hauled the man outside. The camera followed and caught a group of guards beating the man, spitting on him, and pelting him with rocks. He was dragged to a mark application site and ordered to worship Nicolae. When the man refused, he was beheaded.

Vicki stood and motioned for Mark to turn the sound off. "I'm glad you were able to see that. None of you should think that what I'm about to say will make your life easy, or that all your troubles will end. In fact, coming out of that cave and following God could mean trouble for you. Look what it did to Tanya. But the point isn't how much trouble you'll be in, it's about finding and following the truth."

A woman raised a hand. "How did he do that resurrection thing?"

"We're told in the Bible that Satan tries to copy God's miracles so he can deceive people. His power is real, but he's a counterfeit. The Global Community wants you to take an identifying mark and worship the potentate. What people don't realize is that when they do, they forfeit any chance of coming to God.

"I want you to understand what you're getting into before we explain what the Bible really says. The GC will hate you if you believe what we're about to say. They'll want to kill you. Cyrus will probably despise you for turning away. But if you pray with us, you'll make a decision that will literally change you forever."

Vicki gestured to Conrad and whispered in his ear, "I need to talk with Tanya. Can you go over some of the material with them?"

Conrad raised his eyebrows, then smiled. "I'll play The Cube."

While Conrad started the computer

program that clearly explained the truth about Jesus Christ, Vicki found Tanya in the storage room sitting on the floor. Her mother's letter was spread out before her, and tears streaked her cheeks.

"You okay?" Vicki said.

Tanya nodded. "This is the saddest thing. All these years and I had no idea."

She held the letter in the air, but Vicki shook her head. "This is too personal. Ty hasn't even read it yet."

"I want you to. If it hadn't been for you, I might never have known about it."

Vicki took the pages. The paper looked old and smelled musty, but neat handwriting flowed across the lines.

> *Dearest Tanya and Ty,*
>
> *Your father won't let me tell you this, so I'm writing it down, hoping one day I'll find a way to talk to you about the most important thing I've discovered. My heart aches to know I can't share this, but I've been praying for both of you nonstop since I learned the truth.*
>
> *You know I've been writing the Christian ministry I hear on the radio every day and they've sent me materials. I found out that Jesus was more than just a man. He is the Son of God. He died to pay the penalty for*

our sins, a perfect sacrifice. I've asked him to come into my life and change me, and he has.

This means the things your father has taught you aren't true. I was blind to think I could work my way to heaven. No one can. Just one little sin separates us from God forever because he is holy. But I'm so thankful that there is forgiveness, and when God says he forgives us, he does it.

I'm hoping this letter is just for me, that I'll be able to tell you these things in person when your dad is away or when we're alone. But if you do read this, it means that for some reason I'm gone.

Vicki turned the page and thought of her own mother. If she'd written Vicki a letter before the disappearances, this would be what she would have said.

I love you both so much and want to see you in the world to come. If I don't get to tell you these things, I've asked God to bring someone into your lives who knows him personally and can lead you to the truth.

Tanya's mother included some verses and references, then a quote from her favorite radio program. She finished with, *"I love you and know that no matter what happens, God loves and cares about you even more."*

Vicki folded the letter and handed it to Tanya. The girl put it carefully in the envelope, closed it, and looked at Vicki. "God answered my mom's prayers with you."

FOUR

Chicago News

WHEN Vicki rejoined the group in the main computer room, Conrad had finished playing The Cube and was explaining more about a personal relationship with God. Three people from the cave had already slipped to their knees.

Vicki asked Tanya to speak to the people, but the thin woman raised a hand. "If it's okay, could we pray now? I don't want to wait."

Vicki nodded. "You have to understand that just saying some words doesn't make you a believer. But if you really want God to forgive you, pray with me."

All seven of the people from the cave closed their eyes and prayed along with Vicki. "Dear God, I know that I've sinned against you, and I deserve punishment. But right now I want to reach out and receive the gift you're offering me in Jesus Christ. I do believe that he died in my place on the cross and paid the penalty for me. Then he rose again and provided a way for me to spend eternity with you. I turn away from my sin and my belief that I can work my way to you, and I accept your grace. Come into my life now, forgive me, and take control of me. Make me the person you want me to be. In Jesus' name I pray. Amen."

The seven stood, all of them with the mark of the believer. They hugged and shook hands with the others. Vicki was overcome with emotion when Ty embraced Tanya. The Bible taught that angels rejoiced each time someone came to God. Vicki knew there were happy angels watching tonight.

But her joy was mixed with uncertainty. So much had happened since Tanya and Ty had shown up at the Wisconsin safe house, and no one knew how the standoff with Cyrus and the others at the cave would end.

"I guess it's pretty hopeless for my dad," Tanya said as Vicki hugged her.

"God got through to you, didn't he? We'll keep praying he breaks through to your dad."

Lionel Washington met with Jacques alone. The man had been disturbed at news reports from Paris that accused his son of being a religious fanatic. Jacques and the others had been careful to cover their identities when they had moved into the chateau, but the whole group had been put on alert and kept an eye out for anyone snooping around the grounds.

Jacques hadn't eaten since Perryn's execution, and his face looked hollow. Lionel said he had been praying for the man and his wife, and Jacques thanked him.

"Judd told me about your conversation, and I want you to know I appreciate your offer to have us stay," Lionel said.

"It comes from the heart. I believe you could greatly help our cause."

Lionel nodded. "Thanks, but I really think my friends back home need us. We've been gone a long time, and it looks like there might be a chance to return soon."

"If that is what God is calling you to, I support you."

"Yeah, but I think Judd feels bad about Perryn. You know, that your son's death was Judd's fault."

Jacques sat on the grass and rubbed his neck. "Guilt is a terrible motivator. I wouldn't want Judd staying because of that."

"Maybe I'm overstepping—"

"No, I appreciate your interest in your friend. Perhaps I was so upset about Perryn's death that I have pulled Judd into the middle of my grief." Jacques put out a hand, and Lionel helped him up. "I will talk with him. Our chateau is your home for as long as you need it and not a moment longer."

Over the next few days, Vicki and the others watched for Cyrus and any other members of the hidden group as she taught the seven new believers the basics about how to study the Bible. They couldn't believe how wrong they had been about Jesus and the meaning of the prophecies. They ate up the teaching and were in their places early each morning as Vicki, Colin, Becky, and Mark led them in their studies.

Several attempts were made to reach Cyrus by radio, but no one answered. Colin became concerned when Ty revealed that his father kept a supply of explosives in a hidden location. Because of the possible threat, everyone stayed in the underground hideout twenty-four hours a day.

"What would he do with the explosives?" Mark said.

Ty frowned. "Go after whoever threatened us or destroy the hideout. He believes he's going to be using the explosives to build the new earth after Armageddon."

Vicki launched into lessons correcting Cyrus's teaching about the end of the world. The people were glad they could read the passages themselves rather than being told what to believe.

No one said anything to Vicki about leaving the group, but she couldn't stop thinking about it.

On the second day after the group had arrived from the cave, the phone rang and Shelly handed it to Vicki.

"Is it Chloe?" Vicki said.

Shelly frowned. "It's your friend in France."

Vicki's heart melted when she heard Judd's voice. She was so glad he was alive and had called that she forgot her problems for a moment.

Judd told her all that had happened to him and where they were staying. Vicki said they had gotten his e-mail about Perryn's death and that Mark was working on a memorial page on the Web site that would list the names, ages, and even pictures of believers who had given their lives for Christ.

"You should also pray for Chang," Judd said. "He's waiting for word about his parents."

"You met them in New Babylon, didn't you?"

"Yes. Chang's father was really into Carpathia and actually got Chang to take Nicolae's mark. Chang's sister, Ming, has flown to China to find them, but the GC are on a rampage, hauling in unmarked citizens and rounding up Jews for concentration camps."

Vicki gulped. "It's really true then, what's happening to Jews and unmarked people?"

"Yes. You can imagine how Chang must feel, waiting for word about his family. What about you?"

Vicki took a breath and told Judd what had happened with Tanya and her father. Judd listened, asking questions about the cave and Cyrus's beliefs.

"You sure stumbled onto a bunch of weird people," Judd finally said, "but at least some of them have become believers. Are you sure you're all right?"

"I'm fine. We're just waiting for Cyrus to

come back. Judd, there's another problem."
Vicki told him that Mark insisted Vicki
should leave.

"He comes down hard on you after what
we forgave him for? You want me to talk to
him?"

"No, I've been thinking it might be good
to go somewhere else, maybe the other
Wisconsin hideout."

"You could come here," Judd said quickly.

"What?"

Judd described the chateau and the people
living there, then said that Jacques had
invited Vicki to come help them. "We could
work here together. There are plenty of
people who need to know God over here."

"Sounds great. Just being with you would
make it worth the risk. Is Lionel staying?"

"He says he's going back as soon as he can.
Westin too. Look, if you don't come, I'm
headed back there on the next flight."

"I was just thinking of Cheryl in the other
safe house. I promised I'd be there when she
delivered her baby."

Judd sighed. "You should definitely stay.
Maybe the move will be good. I'll meet you
there."

Vicki paused. Though Judd had talked
about the two of them, she wanted to hear

his thoughts again. "You really think there's a future for us?"

When Judd spoke, Vicki closed her eyes and imagined the smile on his face. "I think there's more than a future for us. Vicki, I think about you constantly. I walk by the garden outside or the water, and I wish you were here to share this with me. All the experiences in Israel, New Babylon, Africa, all the places we've been and things we've seen— they all would have been so much better if you would have been with me."

Vicki put a hand to her chest, catching her breath. "Wow. What about that girl you met, Nada?"

"She even sensed what I was feeling. I want to tell you everything. She was courageous, but I don't ever want you to feel that I have any less feelings for you because of what happened between her and me."

Vicki didn't speak and Judd quickly added, "I don't want to scare you or make you think I've gone off the deep end, but with every day that passes I think you and I were meant to be more than just coworkers or friends. Just talking with you has helped me make the decision."

"I should have called you first when all this happened with Mark. Now I feel like no matter what happens here, everything's going to be okay."

"I'll let you know when we get the details about our flight back to the States. Keep us in your prayers."

"Always," Vicki said.

When she hung up, Vicki talked with Becky and found the number for Marshall Jameson, the man who had picked up the others from the safe house. She called and explained her situation, asking if there was any chance she could join them in Avery, Wisconsin.

"We might be able to help you," Marshall said. "We're expecting a new guy straight from the Trib Force any day now."

"What's his name?"

"He goes by Z, but his real name—"

"Zeke?" Vicki said. "I know him!"

"Let me find out when he's supposed to arrive. I'll call you back."

Vicki knew the Trib Force had been head-quartered somewhere in Chicago. To see Zeke again, along with Charlie, Melinda, Janie, and the others in Avery would take some of the sting away from Mark's anger. Still, Vicki wondered what would happen to Tanya, Ty, and the others from the cave.

As she walked into the computer area,

Vicki felt a rumbling, and windows upstairs rattled through the open door. Colin called everyone upstairs to the front window. A huge, smoky cloud rose over the trees to the south, surging in the shape of a mushroom. Vicki had seen pictures in textbooks and on documentaries that looked like this.

Mark called the others downstairs as a special report aired from the Global Community News Network. "We have this word in from the United North American States, where a strategic strike has been leveled on the city of Chicago."

The television switched to a live aerial shot from a plane some distance away showing a closer view of the rising smoke. "We have reports from Global Community officials who estimate at least a thousand casualties on the ground, all believed to be Judah-ites who have made this city their haven. Those numbers, of course, can't be confirmed because of the nuclear fallout. But authorities do believe this was a major victory in the war against rebels who actively fight against the peaceful mission of the Global Community."

Vicki put a hand to her mouth. If the reports were true, Buck Williams, Chloe, Kenny, Zeke, and the other members of the Tribulation Force were all dead.

Sam Goldberg felt like he was experiencing a little bit of heaven each day in Petra. Building continued as people fashioned small homes and shelters throughout the rocky city. Flights from the Trib Force Co-op regularly brought in building supplies. They had no need for food because God provided it on the ground every day.

One afternoon Sam slipped on a rock outcropping and fell to his knees. He was sure he had torn a hole in his pants, but when he stood, his pants were like new again.

Each day Tsion and Micah taught from God's Word, and Sam recorded the messages and included bits and pieces in his Petra Diaries for readers around the world.

> *Today Dr. Ben-Judah concentrated on the prophecies yet to be fulfilled. Many of them made me shudder, like the battle of Armageddon, but others caused my heart to swell. One day our Lord and Savior will return in power and might. One day we will see the new Jerusalem filled with the glory of God and sparkling like a precious jewel. We will view a city of gold, and the Lord God Almighty and the Lamb will be its temple.*

*Think of it. These are not simply words
written in a book. These things we speak of
will actually come true, and you and I, if
we are part of God's forever family, will see
them come true!*

Vicki dreaded the phone call from Marshall
Jameson. She had a sick feeling that the news
would not be good about her move to Avery.
She had told Mark and the others about her
decision to leave. Though Shelly had pro-
tested the most, she said she understood.

Ty Spivey asked permission to go to the
cave and confront his father, but everyone
thought it was too dangerous. Repeated radio
calls to the group remained unanswered.

When the secure phone rang, Vicki's heart
leaped.

Colin answered and handed the phone to
Vicki. "It's for you."

"Hello?" Vicki said.

Instead of Marshall Jameson's voice, a
familiar female voice answered. "Vicki. It's
Chloe."

FIVE

Chloe Steele Williams

VICKI was elated to hear Chloe's voice and to discover that the Tribulation Force was alive and well. Chloe, Buck, and their son, Kenny, had gotten out of the city three days before the blast had leveled Chicago.

Chloe told Vicki the latest about Kenny—how old he was and some of the things he was doing and saying. The boy missed his "Uncle" Tsion and Zeke. Buck was working on his cyberzine, *The Truth,* and enjoying watching Kenny grow. They all missed Dr. Ben-Judah but understood that he had to be in Petra.

"My dad is still there," Chloe said. "The things going on are incredible."

Vicki told Chloe about Sam Goldberg and his Petra Diaries, and Chloe said she would read them. Chloe told Vicki more about their middle-of-the-night departure from Chicago. "It was scary not knowing when the bomb would fall, but we managed to get everyone out in time."

"No one has been caught by the GC?"

"We did lose a good friend a few days ago," Chloe said. "A guy Buck used to work for, Steve Plank. He became a believer and assumed a new identity inside the Global Community. He was the one responsible for the release of Hattie Durham from the GC and was the first to tell us we should leave Chicago."

"What happened to him?" Vicki said.

"He didn't have Nicolae's mark so they came for him. Steve could have run, but he said his time was up. We watched a live feed from Colorado. You should have seen how brave he was as they led him to the guillotine."

Chloe asked Vicki what had happened to her since they had last talked. It felt like talking to a big sister, though Vicki had never had one. Chloe gasped when she heard about the rescue in Iowa, the raid at the schoolhouse, the courage of Natalie Bishop and Manny Aguilara, and Vicki's daring attempt to reach young people during the GC's worldwide youth meetings.

"I haven't read your Web site lately

because of the operation in Greece," Chloe said, "but I remember—"

"You were involved in that?" Vicki interrupted.

"Yes. It was pretty scary going face-to-face with the GC and running through the countryside to rescue our friend, but I can honestly say I felt God was with us."

"You got the guy out?"

"He freed himself, and we made it to the airplane. That's where things got really interesting."

Chloe described seeing a real angel on the plane and how he had blinded GC officials chasing the rescue team. "From what Tsion says, I think we're going to be seeing a lot more of that type of thing in the future."

"You mean angels?"

"The Scriptures talk about the deception of Antichrist and his false prophet. But in the future there's going to be even more of it. I don't know what form it will take, but you can bet Nicolae will use anything and everything he can to trick people into believing he's really God."

Chloe asked about Vicki's travels across the country, and Vicki described their attempt to reach young people. When Vicki told Chloe what had happened to them in Arizona,

Vicki realized she had never told Buck Williams that she had met his brother.

"You knew Buck's brother and father were killed in a fire, didn't you?" Chloe said.

"Yes, and I was there just before Jeff became a believer."

Chloe put Buck on the phone, and Vicki told him everything she could remember. Buck was silent through much of the story, but Vicki could tell he was emotional when she finished.

"He made me promise I wouldn't tell anybody about him," Vicki said. "He even told me I couldn't get in touch with you."

"He was so worried about my safety, but he didn't take care of himself."

Buck thanked Vicki and put Chloe back on the phone. Vicki asked where the Tribulation Force had relocated, and Chloe told her about a series of homes and safe houses around the country where people had gone. "We discovered a hidden group of believers in Chicago, and they've gone all over. I'm in California in an underground bunker that used to be a military base. Zeke had moved in with us in Chicago after his father was killed, and he's off to—"

"Avery, Wisconsin," Vicki said. She told Chloe how she knew and that she was probably going to the same place. Vicki paused. "I have a question about . . . well . . . when you and Buck got together and then had little Kenny. Did anyone think it was wrong to start a family during the Tribulation?"

Chloe laughed. "I suppose there were people who thought the times were too tough for romance. And some said it was foolish to bring up a child at this time. Tsion quoted a famous author who said, 'A baby is God's way of saying he wants the world to go on.' I'll admit I wasn't ready for marriage at the time of the disappearances, but believing in Christ changed me. It made me more mature."

"So you don't have any regrets?"

"About marriage? None. Things are hard at times. Buck and I butt heads, and it would be easier to make decisions on my own instead of being accountable to another person, but I can't imagine life without him. We're a team. Why do you ask?"

Vicki told Chloe about Judd.

"He's pretty cute, as I recall," Chloe said.

Vicki blushed. "We've butted heads a lot too. You don't think that's a problem?"

"If you're fighting constantly it might be. My guess is, with the time you've spent apart, you're different people. You've both grown, and if you're still interested in him it's a good sign."

"But I want to give my life to God. Wouldn't having a relationship like this distract me from serving him?"

"If it were a wrong relationship, you bet. But if God is calling you together, it could make you even more effective." Chloe sighed. "When I was younger my mom encouraged me to follow God and only date believers. I thought a Christian wouldn't want to have fun. I thought life would be boring. Now I know the truth, and I can see why it's important to be married to a true believer."

"I can't imagine the pain of being married to a Carpathia follower," Vicki said. "But what about the verses that say it's better to stay single?"

"God is the one who set up marriage, and he said it was good. Believe me, I looked up verses and asked questions just like you're doing. I love the one in Proverbs where it says, 'The man who finds a wife finds a treasure and receives favor from the Lord.' I remind Buck all the time what a treasure he has, and he doesn't argue."

Vicki laughed.

"Everybody is different," Chloe continued, "and I think you need to stay close to God. If being married is one of the desires he's put on your heart, he'll work it out."

"We haven't had much opportunity to talk, other than on the phone," Vicki said. "He's stuck in France."

"Really? Where in France?"

Vicki told her and Chloe clicked a keyboard. "I'm looking at our Co-op flights. We don't have a whole lot going through that part of the world, but there's a load of supplies I diverted sitting in a warehouse in Saarbrücken, a few hours east of where Judd is. Chang might not know about that."

"Can you get Judd back here?"

"He'd have to go by way of Petra and then take another flight home, probably to South Carolina."

"We have friends there," Vicki said. "I'm sure Judd wouldn't mind seeing Petra. When did you say the flight is?"

"Petra needs the materials right away. The plane is scheduled to be there in two days— it'll only stop long enough to load and then head out."

Chloe said it wouldn't be a problem to include Lionel and Westin on the flight. "Have Westin write me with his experience and we'll see if we can't get him a plane."

Vicki talked about moving to Avery, and Chloe said the decision was up to Vicki. "As long as you can get there safely, I don't see a problem."

Vicki wrote down Judd's flight information and sent him an urgent e-mail. She couldn't believe one phone call had answered so many questions.

Judd threw a fist in the air when he got Vicki's e-mail.

Westin immediately fired off a message to Chloe outlining his flying experience. "Two days and we're out of here!" he said.

Judd found Jacques in the chateau study. The man took off his glasses and welcomed Judd. "I was just reading one of the Psalms. I would never have thought that simple words on a page could mean so much."

Jacques slipped his glasses on and held the book open. "Listen to this. 'My enemy has chased me. He has knocked me to the ground. He forces me to live in darkness like those in the grave.'" He looked up. "Believers today know exactly how David felt. And listen to this. 'Save me from my enemies, Lord; I run to you to hide me. Teach me to do your will, for you are my God. May your gracious Spirit lead me forward on a firm footing. For the glory of your name, O Lord, save me.'"

Jacques closed his Bible. "That was from Psalm 143. As I read, I thought of Perryn, how he must have prayed right before the end. And God used his death, I'm sure, for his glory."

Judd looked at the floor and cracked his knuckles. "We just got an e-mail. Do you know where Saarbrücken is?"

"Yes, I have relatives from that area. We used to go there as a family."

"There's a Co-op plane coming. We think we've found a way back to the States."

Jacques smiled broadly, threw out his arms, and embraced Judd. When he let go, the man's eyes were filled with tears. "My wife and I have prayed that God would show you what to do. I rejoice that he has answered so quickly."

Mark helped Colin prepare for the worst outside his Wisconsin home. Though they had video surveillance, Colin worried that the group from the cave might try to attack and rescue their own members. It made no sense, of course, but there was nothing about the group that *did* make sense.

Mark was glad Vicki had taken his concerns seriously, but now that she was leaving, he felt troubled. The seven new believers were growing, and Vicki seemed to be truly sorry about putting the group in danger.

"You were probably too hard on her, but she's made her decision," Colin said when Mark confided in him. "I believe God can use even the problems we have with each other."

"What do you mean?" Mark said.

"The disciples had squabbles, and even Paul and Barnabas had a fight over John Mark. They were human, and God uses humans for his purposes, working things out for his glory."

Vicki had just gotten off the phone with Marshall Jameson when Mark walked into the computer room. "It's set. Marshall is picking me up tomorrow and taking whoever wants to go to Avery. Ty and Tanya are definitely coming."

Mark nodded. "About Judd, I was thinking that you should write Tom and Luke Gowin in South Carolina—"

"Got a message back from them about an

hour ago," Vicki said. "They're sending Judd directions and a place to meet them after they land."

"Seems like things are all set then," Mark said as he turned to leave.

"Did you want something else?"

Mark sighed. "I still think it was wrong for you to go out there, but seeing the way the new people are learning . . . I'm sorry I was so hard on you."

Vicki put a hand on Mark's arm. "We've been together a long time. I deserved to be chewed out. I think moving in with the others will be good for me, and Colin's letting us take one of his high-powered laptops."

"Sweet."

An alarm rang at the computer, and people came running. Conrad switched to the full-screen view as several men walked toward the house from the woods.

SIX

Mysterious Stranger

VICKI watched the safe house go into crisis mode with people scurrying to secure the upstairs and lock themselves underground. Colin had warned the new believers that this might happen if Cyrus returned.

Vicki feared the men would break in and trash Colin and Becky's home. They would never find the combination that unlocked the downstairs door, but Vicki wasn't sure what dynamite would do to the entrance.

Everyone stood before the monitor as Mark switched from one camera to the next for the best view.

"That looks like my dad out in front," Tanya said.

Becky, Shelly, and a few new arrivals huddled in a corner and prayed. Vicki heard one of them ask God to "soften Prophet Cy's heart."

Tanya edged closer to Vicki and trembled as she whispered, "I always thought Dad loved us, but I can see now that he's mixed up."

"Your dad controls people."

"Yeah, it's like he put people under a spell. Ty and I were kids, so we were easy. But the others are adults. They should have known better."

"People like to be told what to believe so they don't have to think. Your dad came along when these people wanted answers."

"But he really believes what he's saying."

"I know, and that makes him even more dangerous."

The men were past the trees now and headed for the house. Vicki glanced at Colin as he set his jaw and put an arm around his wife.

The radio crackled. "I'd like to talk with my people."

Colin held up a hand. "Let's see what happens if we don't respond."

Mark zoomed in on the leader when the man put the walkie-talkie to his lips again. "I'm sure you can hear me, so talk. If you don't, I'll assume you're holding them against their will. By now, they've no doubt seen how wrong they were to leave."

Tanya looked at Colin. "Could I say something to him?"

Colin handed her the radio. "Just don't tell him where we are."

Mark pointed at a man walking toward the group from the shadows. "What's this guy doing?"

Ty studied the screen. "I've never seen him before."

"Stay calm," Colin said to Tanya.

Tanya took a breath and keyed the microphone. "Dad, it's me."

"Are you all right, honey?"

"I'm fine. They have food here, and they're really nice."

"Is Ty there?"

"Ty's with me." She named the others in the group and said they were rested and well fed.

"Well, it's time for everybody to come on back," Cyrus said. "The others are welcome too. You'd best get out before the big push to Armageddon."

"Dad, we've been watching the news and listening to reports from the Middle East. You're wrong about Armageddon. It's not

going to happen for more than three years.
Petra was attacked, but the people survived."

"Don't let those people brainwash you,
Tanya. I've warned you about that. Now
come out and we'll forget this ever happened."

One of the men stepped toward Cyrus and
handed him something. "I know you can see
me through your little cameras," Cyrus said,
holding the object up. "We've got enough
dynamite out here to blow your place sky-
high. I suggest you listen and get out now."

Colin grabbed the radio. "Mr. Spivey, the
only thing we've done is take some of your
followers in, feed them, and help them
understand the truth."

"Evidently you don't think I mean business." Cyrus turned. "Hand me the lighter."

"He's going to throw that at the house,"
Mark said. "Are we safe?"

"There are several layers of concrete
underground, but the ceiling isn't as thick,"
Colin said.

Cyrus took the lighter and held the dynamite over his head. "Last chance."

"You'll hurt your own people if you throw
that in here," Colin said into the radio.

"We should get out," Tanya said. "Is there
a back way?"

Several scrambled for the door, but Colin

yelled for them to stop. In the confusion, Vicki noticed the stranger in the shadows step forward. He pushed his way through the others until he stood next to the leader.

"Who are you?" Cyrus said.

The man took the dynamite from Cyrus and dropped it on the ground. Two of Cyrus's followers moved toward the mystery man.

Vicki studied him carefully. He had a short beard and wore what looked like a long, flowing robe. When Cyrus's men reached him, he put up a hand, and the two fell to the ground.

The man looked past Cyrus toward the house. "Come out."

His voice reverberated through the underground hideout, and Vicki looked at the others. "I think he means us."

Cyrus stumbled back a few feet when the man spoke again. "Everyone come out." He looked at Cyrus. "Send someone for the others in your group."

"H-how do you know about my people?" Cyrus stammered.

"Go."

One of the men staggered into the woods and ran away. Vicki's heart raced, and Tanya and the other new believers whimpered.

Everyone knew something strange was happening.

"Don't be afraid," the man said. "Come out."

Colin unlocked the door that led upstairs. "Everybody follow me."

Tanya caught Vicki's arm as they walked upstairs. "Who is that?"

"I don't know, but I think we'll be all right."

They moved outside and approached the group. Cyrus, who had seemed so confident, now cowered with the others.

"Come closer and listen carefully," the man said in a soft voice. He didn't have an accent, and though he didn't speak loudly, everyone seemed able to hear.

"Tanya, get over here," Cyrus said. The man looked at him, and Cyrus grew wide-eyed with fear.

Vicki noticed the man wore sandals instead of shoes. He was about the same height as Colin and had dark hair.

He turned and stared straight at Vicki. "My name is Anak. I have been sent by the Holy One, the true God and Father of our Lord and Savior, Jesus the Messiah. I have a message of warning. You and your fellow believers are in grave danger. You must leave this place at once."

Jesus Christ, is ready to give you eternal life, but you must first stop your striving for perfection. Your righteous acts are like filthy rags. Your faith is strong, but you have not placed your faith in the one who died to redeem you. Worship the true and living God. Fear him and give glory to him."

Anak paused as a few of the people fell to their knees. Vicki wanted to turn and run, to obey Anak's warning, but her feet felt glued to the ground.

Anak put out his hands as if he were pleading. "As you have heard from the young one, Christ died for your sins according to the Scriptures; he was buried, and he rose again the third day. Now turn from your sins and turn to God, so you can be cleansed of your sins. There is no judgment awaiting those who trust him. But those who do not trust him have already been judged for not believing in the only Son of God. Their judgment is based on this fact: The light from heaven came into the world, but they loved the darkness more than the light, for their actions were evil."

"Are you . . . from the . . . Global Community?" Cyrus said.

Anak gritted his teeth and his eyes flashed. "If any man worships the beast and his image, and receives his mark on his forehead or in his hand, that one shall drink of the wine of the wrath of God, which is poured out into the cup of his indignation. The one with the mark shall be tormented with fire and brimstone in the presence of the holy angels and in the presence of the Lamb, who is Christ the Messiah.

"The smoke of his torment ascends forever and ever, and he will have no rest day or night, he who worships the beast and his image and receives the mark of his name."

Cyrus was clearly shaken. He glanced at Tanya and Ty with a look of disgust, as if they'd done something wrong. He gestured to the others to head back to the cave, and everyone slowly followed.

"Today you must listen to his voice," Anak pleaded. "Don't harden your hearts against him."

Two of Cyrus's followers turned back and fell at Anak's feet. "Do not worship me, for I am a created being. Worship God in spirit and in truth."

Anak knelt with the two and whispered. When he rose, the two had the mark of the true believer on their foreheads.

"Go and join your new family," Anak said, pointing to Vicki and the others. "And now, all glory to God, who is able to keep you from stumbling and who will bring you into his glorious presence innocent of sin and with great joy. All glory to him, who alone is God our Savior, through Jesus Christ our Lord. Yes, glory, majesty, power, and authority belong to him, in the beginning, now, and forevermore. Amen."

Vicki looked at Tanya, who was so moved she couldn't speak. When Vicki turned, Anak stood next to her. "You will see your friends again before the Glorious Appearing of the King of kings and Lord of lords. But one you love will see much pain and will not return whole."

"What do you mean?" Vicki whispered.

But Anak was gone. Like a breath of wind, he vanished.

"What do we do now?" Ty said to Colin.

Colin counted heads. "We put our stuff in the vehicles and leave. Now."

SEVEN

Mark's Dangerous Idea

JUDD called Chang for an update, and Chang assured him that the reports about Judah-ite deaths in Chicago were false. Judd asked about their flight, and Chang said he would relay the departure time and pilot's name soon.

"So all the Trib Force got out of Chicago?"

"Yes, but they're scattered to the wind. Some in California, others in some western suburbs of Chicago, one in a remote section of Wisconsin. But something is brewing in the States right now, and I haven't been able to figure it out."

"What do you mean?"

"I've told you about this before. I've intercepted several e-mails between top officials there and New Babylon, especially from this new guy, Commander Fulcire. They're starting a new program in the States, but I don't know what it is."

"Any news about your parents?"

"Not yet. And there's a lot of GC activity in China that concerns me."

After Judd hung up, he read the latest Petra Diaries from Sam Goldberg and was thrilled about the way God had protected and provided for the people there. God had done the same for the Young Trib Force for the last three and a half years. And Judd prayed that would continue.

Mark knew what he had to do as soon as he heard Anak's warning, but he didn't know if Colin would agree. After the angel vanished, Mark retrieved the sticks of dynamite Cyrus and the others had dropped and ran for the house. Colin and Becky were backing the vehicles out of the garage, and people were filling trash bags with clothes, food, and supplies and throwing them inside.

"Everybody in!" Colin yelled.

Mark ran to Colin and opened the van door, out of breath. "The computers have all of—"

"We don't have time to take the system apart. I've got the laptops."

"If Anak was warning us about the Global Community, and I think he was, and they find your place and the computer setup, our Web site and all of our contacts will be discovered."

Colin's eyes darted from Mark to his house.

"Your contact in Avery, the people who sent your equipment, the GC will find all of it," Mark continued. "They'll have access to every e-mail address in our database, everybody who has written us or we've sent The Cube to."

People jammed into the van and Becky's car.

Finally, Colin got out. "What's your plan?"

Mark held up the dynamite. "This. It'll probably save lives."

"What if it's not the GC?"

"Are you willing to risk it? If it is the GC, we'll never come back here."

Colin reached for the dynamite, but Mark shook his head. "It was my idea. Take the cars to the end of the driveway and I'll meet you there."

"No. We do this together and we do it right."

Colin quickly talked with his wife, who leaned against the car, overcome with what he planned to do. Finally, Colin hurried into the house while Becky and one of the new believers drove everyone toward the road.

"Four sticks downstairs, two upstairs," Colin said.

"How long will these fuses burn?"

"Thirty seconds. Maybe a minute. You take the upstairs, and I'll do the computer area."

Mark's stomach churned. He knew what they were about to do was dangerous. One mistake could mean their lives.

Colin took a final look around the house and sighed. "We put a lot of work in this place. It's hard to see it go."

Mark handed him four sticks of dynamite and a lighter. Colin raced downstairs, lighting the four fuses at the same time. Mark lit the other two sticks, threw one on the kitchen floor, and carried the other down the hall.

Colin flew up the stairs and ran through the back door. "Hurry up!"

Mark tossed the other stick in a bedroom and raced for the front door full force but it stuck, the doorframe cracking as he plowed into it. A series of latches was locked, and Mark knew he didn't have time to open them. He ran through the kitchen again to the back door.

How many seconds had elapsed since Colin first lit the explosives in the basement?

Ten? Twenty? Mark heard Colin calling his name as he sprinted through the back door. His legs felt like jelly. He had run on the track team in high school and prided himself on being a good runner, but now his legs moved in slow motion, not responding to the urgency of the moment.

Mark tripped on a slope in the yard and went down hard, knocking the air from his lungs. He was only a few steps from the house. *I should just lay here*, he thought. He covered his head with his hands and waited for the explosion.

Vicki ran a hand across Becky's photo album and looked back at the house. Becky had told the group what Colin planned to do, and Vicki was glad everyone had taken Anak's warning seriously.

"Does this kind of thing happen a lot?" a new believer said.

Vicki rolled her eyes. "Not very often, thankfully."

Colin appeared from the back of the house, turned, and ran back. Becky yelled for him as he disappeared. Then Vicki spotted him on the driveway, dragging Mark beside him.

A terrific explosion rocked the van and Vicki

ducked. When she looked again, fire and smoke rose from the house. Colin and Mark were nowhere in sight. Splinters of wood, brick, and concrete rained down on the van. Another explosion. Vicki took a second look at the house and couldn't believe her eyes. The whole thing had disintegrated.

"Colin!" Becky screamed as she rushed from the van.

Everyone followed and ran toward the inferno. Vicki's heart sank when Colin called for Mark from a drainage ditch by the driveway.

Sam Goldberg spent his time on the computer or building tents and small homes in Petra. Every hour he found new people and things to write about in his Petra Diaries. There were stories of deliverance and miracles of God, and the Almighty was providing for every need.

But one thing nagged Sam. He had known Naomi Tiberius for a long time, even before coming to Petra. She always seemed so much older, but now after working closely on the computer system, Sam couldn't help thinking of her as more than a friend. She was beautiful, and though Sam was years younger, he couldn't stop thinking about her. Naomi seemed to value his opinion and treat him with respect.

As Sam munched on his morning manna in his small tent, he wondered if Naomi could feel the same way about him. Could she want to be more than friends?

Every time Naomi spoke of Chang Wong, Sam felt jealous. She talked about him like he was some sort of miracle worker. True, Chang was in constant danger in New Babylon, but he had volunteered for the job.

Sam closed his eyes and practiced what he would say to Naomi the next time he saw her. *"I know I'm younger than you, but I'm mature for my age."*

No, that sounded too much like begging. He had to be sure of himself. *"Naomi, I'd like to ask your father if we could date."*

Sam sighed. He couldn't imagine even talking to Naomi's father, let alone asking if he could take out the man's daughter. And where would they go?

That's it, Sam thought. *I'll ask if we could sit together during Tsion's next message.*

Sam sat on his cot. *But she'll see right through me. And if I explain my true feelings it'll scare her away. Better to keep quiet and save my dignity than open my mouth and lose it.*

But what if she feels the same way about me? I could be missing my chance by keeping quiet.

Sam finished his breakfast wondering if he would have the courage to speak with Naomi later.

Vicki and the others helped Mark and Colin out of the ditch and to the vehicles. Colin was groggy from the blast and couldn't drive, so he rode in the passenger seat.

Vicki went with Mark in Becky's car and held a finger to his wrist. "He has a pulse," she said. "Maybe he's just knocked out."

Mark had scratches on his face from his fall, and the back of his clothes were scorched from the heat of the explosion. Vicki found fragments of wood in Mark's hair and brushed them out.

When they reached a curve in the road, Shelly pointed at the house. What had been their high-tech hideout was only a smoking hole in the ground.

Mark mumbled something, and Vicki put a hand under his head. "What did you say?"

"Did we get rid of everything?" Mark croaked.

"You did good," Conrad said. "Almost got yourself killed though."

Mark muttered something about a locked door, and Becky handed Vicki an emergency kit from the glove compartment. "There's some pain reliever in one of the bottles. Give him two tablets. Everybody keep down. I see some cars heading our way."

A walkie-talkie squawked. Colin had installed radios in each vehicle weeks earlier. "Is that you, hon?" Becky said.

"Birnbaums," Colin said. "Stay quiet."

"Who are the Birnbaums?" Vicki said.

"Neighbors who used to live around here," Becky said.

The van made a sharp left turn up a tree-lined driveway and Becky followed. After they stopped out of sight of the road, Becky got out and rushed to the van. Vicki rolled down her window and heard Becky ask Colin if he was all right.

"Shh," Colin said. "Those cars look official. Could be GC."

Vicki heard the whir of tires on asphalt. Colored lights swirled, the reflection shining on trees, and a large truck with a satellite dish on top passed. Had Anak's warning come too late?

"Get out of here," Colin said. "Only use the radio if you have to. They might be monitoring all frequencies."

Becky turned the car around and slowly drove to the road with her lights off. The van followed close behind as they headed west.

Lionel Washington watched GCNN's latest news coverage and found a channel devoted exclusively to events coming from the United North American States. He wanted to know not only what was going on back in his home country, but what to expect when they arrived.

Lionel couldn't wait to get back. He wondered if everyone had changed as much as he had. He had grown taller since being away and had tried to grow a beard without much success. He had also put on some muscle and felt leaner.

Lionel was excited about Westin's new role in the Co-op. Chloe Williams had already teamed him up with another pilot. He would fly from Petra to a location in Argentina while Judd and Lionel waited for their ride to South Carolina. Lionel knew it would be difficult saying good-bye to their friend. But he was glad the man had escaped Z-Van and the Global Community and looked forward to hearing of his travels for the Tribulation Force.

Judd had studied the e-mail from Luke, Tom, and Carl in South Carolina and knew the plan by heart. After what Lionel and Judd had been through the past few weeks, Lionel hoped they might stay near the ocean before heading north to their friends.

A special bulletin flashed and Lionel sat up. A crawl at the bottom reported a Judah-ite hideout had been discovered in Wisconsin and that more details would follow. A few minutes later, the anchor introduced April Wojekowski who was live at the scene of another GC raid.

"Peter, as you can see behind me there is nothing left of this Judah-ite hideout except a hole in the ground and splintered wood. GC authorities are combing the site for clues to those who were inside when the building exploded. We don't know yet if this was a Global Community air strike, or if it was the work of sabotage. What we do know is—and I've been told this by the commander working this investigation—that the Global Community saw recent activity here through satellite surveillance, and that . . ."

April turned and waved a hand. Her microphone wagged back and forth, and a man in uniform walked into the picture. "This is Commander Kruno Fulcire, who is the head of the Rebel Apprehension Program. Commander, what can you tell us?"

"Well, these were definitely Judah-ites with some advanced computer equipment. Because of the amount of weapons stashed inside and the threat of a battle, we had to dismantle the hideout with explosives. If you'll look over there, you'll see the remaining group who were captured in a cave not far from here."

Lionel held his breath as he strained to see the darkened faces of people being led to a GC van. He didn't recognize anyone and wondered if Vicki and the others were alive.

EIGHT

Back with Friends

JUDD felt sick as he watched the news coverage from the Wisconsin raid. He tried calling and e-mailing Vicki, but there was no response. He did get a quick message back from Darrion, who was staying in another Wisconsin location.

We got a phone call saying Vicki and some others were coming this way, Darrion wrote, *but we haven't heard anything since.*

"Who were the people being taken away?" Lionel said.

Judd guessed it might be the people from the cave Vicki had talked about. He was glad he hadn't recognized anyone in custody, but he felt saddened by the faces of those without the mark of Carpathia or God.

Chang Wong didn't know anything more about the raid than what they had seen on

GCNN, but he said he wouldn't be surprised if the GC stepped up their search for believers. "This Fulcire guy is known for his brutal treatment of prisoners. He comes across as fair and caring on TV, but I wouldn't want him to catch me."

The news also reported Z-Van's travels. He had sung to a mammoth crowd in Madrid, Spain, after the Paris concert, dazzling spectators with his music and high-flying antics. No one on TV questioned *how* Z-Van was able to hover over the stage and perform his act, but Judd knew it was more than trickery.

A parallel story about Lars Rahlmost showed the man finishing his documentary of Nicolae Carpathia's rise. The filmmaker was also working on a companion book that would show world reaction to Nicolae's resurrection, detailing where people were and what they were doing the moment they heard Nicolae was alive again.

Jacques gathered the entire group and asked everyone to pray for Vicki and the other believers with her. Judd felt a surge of emotion as he listened to the prayers in French. He could understand only a few words, but the intent was clear. These people cared for their brothers and sisters in Christ no matter where they were.

Jacques prayed for Chang Wong's sister

and parents, then asked God to protect their own group as they drove to the meeting place in Saarbrücken. "Deliver your servants safely back to their friends," he prayed, "and use us in your service."

There were hugs and tears as Judd, Lionel, and Westin got in Jacques' car. Jacques' wife kissed Judd on both cheeks and said something in French.

"She is quoting from a passage from Colossians she used to pray for Perryn," Jacques said. "We ask God to give you a complete understanding of what he wants to do in your lives, and we ask him to make you wise with spiritual wisdom. Then the way you live will always honor and please the Lord, and you will continually do good, kind things for others. All the while, you will learn to know God better and better."

Vicki kept an eye on Mark as they drove. Becky sat behind the wheel wiping away tears. Vicki felt sorry for the woman. Everything she owned had just been blasted to smithereens, and Vicki felt responsible. If she hadn't gone after Tanya, Colin and Becky would still be in their home.

Vicki was glad Tanya was riding with them.

The girl sat in front of Vicki, her shoulders shaking. When Mark leaned against the window and fell asleep, Vicki touched Tanya's shoulder. "Anything I can do?"

Tanya turned and put her chin on the headrest. "I keep thinking about Dad and the others. Why didn't they believe what the angel said?"

Vicki frowned. "Your dad bought into something that's not the truth, and it's keeping him from understanding what a relationship with God really is."

"What's going to happen to them?"

"Maybe they'll come to their senses like the others and believe."

"Or the GC could—"

Becky motioned from the front. "Sorry to interrupt, but listen to this." She turned up the radio and caught the newscaster mid-sentence. ". . . were taken into custody and are being questioned by authorities in what is being described as a successful raid at a Judah-ite encampment. Commander Kruno Fulcire was on-site and had this to say."

"Fulcire," Shelly said. "That's the same guy who was chasing us in Iowa!"

"So far we've discovered a stash of weapons and plans to carry out terrorist acts against the Global Community and the general popula-tion," Fulcire said. "We've found guns, ammunition, dynamite, large quantities of fuel, and complex communication devices. This adds more proof to the growing mountain of evidence that these Judah-ites are against peace. Anyone who suspects another citizen of being a Judah-ite or simply not taking the mark of our lord and king, Nicolae Carpathia, can call or e-mail us anonymously and we'll check the people out.

"I might add that the citizens of this fine region can sleep easier tonight knowing the Global Community has gotten rid of such violent people."

The newscaster told where the group was being taken and said if they did not take Carpathia's mark, they would face the guillotine.

"Sorry that was such bad news," Becky said, turning down the volume.

"It won't matter if Dad and the others take the mark now," Tanya said, bowing her head. "If they don't believe in God there's no hope."

"I wonder if Ty knows," Vicki said.

The car and van continued west, with Colin pointing out the best route. Vicki closed her eyes and thought of Anak. When she had first seen him, he looked like just another man, but the more he talked, the more she could see the difference. His face seemed to glow with the knowledge of God. Who knew how many people he had warned or how many places he had been in the past few years?

Vicki had felt strangely warmed by the angel's words about her and the Young Trib Force. *So much for God being silent,* Vicki thought. Still, something Anak had said troubled her. *"But one you love will see much pain and will not return whole."*

What did that mean? Were his words a prediction of Mark's injury? Was something bad going to happen to Judd? Vicki sat back and watched the miles roll by. She prayed for wisdom and clear understanding.

Sam sat in the computer class listening to Naomi explain how to answer questions on Tsion Ben-Judah's Web site. He tried to concentrate but was stuck on Naomi's face. He hadn't noticed before how striking her eyes were and the way her hair accented her beauty.

As others left for the day's session with Dr. Ben-Judah, Naomi caught Sam staring at her. "What is it?"

Sam coughed. "Nothing. I mean, I was just thinking about Tsion's message. It would be nice to sit with someone I know."

"You mean someone from the class?"

"No. I mean, yes. I was thinking you could tell me more about how to use the computers."

"Sam, you already know as much as you need. I've seen you sending your Petra Diaries."

Sam blushed. "Really? What do you think of my writing?"

"It's cute."

Cute? Sam thought. *Puppies are cute. A child's drawing is cute.*

Naomi smiled. "I generally sit with my father, who sits with the elders. You can sit with us if you'd like."

"Thanks, but I'm okay," he said.

Sam waited until Naomi left, then walked along a ledge overlooking the red rock city. He had to forget Naomi and focus on what was important.

The morning sun was hot when Tsion Ben-Judah stood before the crowd. While other believers around the world were starved for interaction with fellow believers, it felt like Sam attended church every day. Dr. Ben-Judah and Micah read from the Bible, talked about what God was teaching them, and always referred to current events. The audience viewed news transmissions that detailed

Nicolae Carpathia's actions. The crowd mostly watched in silence but couldn't help booing and jeering the foul words of the evil man.

Tsion began his message with a plea to those who were still undecided about Jesus Christ. He showed prophecy after prophecy that Jesus had fulfilled and asked believers to pray for these undecided.

"My main teaching comes from the book of Isaiah, chapter 43. Listen to the Word of the Lord. 'But now, O Israel, the Lord who created you says: "Do not be afraid, for I have ransomed you. I have called you by name; you are mine. When you go through deep waters and great trouble, I will be with you. When you go through rivers of difficulty, you will not drown! When you walk through the fire of oppression, you will not be burned up; the flames will not consume you. For I am the Lord, your God, the Holy One of Israel, your Savior."'

"We see here a picture of a God of unfailing love. Even though Israel has turned her back on him, even though they have followed others and gone their own way, God has been faithful to his promise to gather his children from every corner of the earth.

"Do not think that when trials and hardship come to your life that God has abandoned you. When you experience these deep waters and the heat of the fire, remember that these are for your good. The deep water is not designed to drown, but to cleanse. The fire will not consume—it is meant to refine."

Tsion continued talking about God's love for the Jewish people and how God was calling Israel to praise him. Great shouts rose from hundreds of thousands and echoed off the rock walls.

When it was time, Micah rose and picked up from the book of Isaiah. Sam didn't know if the two had coordinated their talk or if it was something they had done without planning, but the effect was one seamless message of love and grace.

"Now I must speak of something that weighs heavy on my heart," Micah said. "I have spoken with many of you who have loved ones who are not here, who have not yet, as far as you know, accepted this grace and love offered by God. It grieves you, as it does me, that these precious ones have yet to believe the truth."

From his perch high above Petra, Sam scanned the crowd. Many people wept, nodding, closing their eyes, or putting a hand in the air. Sam spotted Rabbi Ben-Eliezar and his wife, who had recently become believers in Christ. Sam knew that their sons weren't believers and the Ben-Eliezars hadn't spoken with them for a long time.

"Please do not give up on your loved ones," Micah continued. "Keep praying. Talk with them if you can. Until they take the mark of Carpathia and worship the beast's image, it is not too late.

"From Isaiah we read these words. 'You have been chosen to know me, believe in me, and understand that I alone am God. There is no other God; there never has been and never will be. I am the Lord, and there is no other Savior.'

"My friends, he is our only hope in this time of great tribulation. And he is the only hope for your family and friends.

"And finally, a word to the young people among us. This message is not just for those who are older. Young people have a great opportunity to praise God and tell others of his love.

"In fact, in the Scriptures we read these words from the apostle Paul. 'Don't let anyone think less of you because you are young. Be an example to all believers in what you teach, in the way you live, in your love, your faith, and your purity.' So no matter what age you are, no matter how long you have believed in the true God of Israel, let us come before him now with those we know who still are outside the fold, and let us pray."

Hundreds of thousands prayed aloud, their words rumbling through the canyon. Sam closed his eyes. "Dear Father, I ask that you help me find the Ben-Eliezar brothers, wherever they are, and that you would help me communicate the truth to them so they would come to know you."

Vicki was exhausted when the two vehicles arrived in Avery, Wisconsin. Charlie bounded out with Phoenix and gave Vicki a hug. The others welcomed the new believers, and everyone gathered in the main cabin.

Colin and Mark greeted each other for the first time after the blast that had leveled Colin's home. Mark smiled and shook his head. "If you hadn't pulled me up, I'd be in a million pieces right now."

Vicki's old friend Zeke found her and welcomed her to the group. He had been there only a short while but had settled in and liked the people. "We have to talk once you're rested," Zeke said.

The leader of the group, Marshall Jameson, called for quiet and asked Colin to explain what had happened. Colin told the story, and people gasped when he came to the message of Anak.

"What did he say?" Zeke said.

Colin nodded to Vicki and she repeated Anak's words, then described what Mark and Colin had done to the house.

"The GC won't find anything bigger than a splinter about us," Conrad said.

People clapped, but Charlie looked concerned. He raised a hand. "What's going to keep the GC from coming here?"

"Good question," Marshall said. "From what we know, this Fulcire guy pinpointed your location by satellite, checking movement on the ground. They probably didn't know what they were going to find when they got there, but discovering people without Carpathia's mark made a good show. You can be sure they'll be doing more of that, which is why we have coverings between our cabins. We're a lot more remote here than you were, but we still have to be careful."

Tanya raised a hand. "Have you heard anything about my dad and the others?"

Marshall pawed the floor with a boot and put his hands behind his back. "I'm afraid we have some bad news. About an hour ago the

GC showed a live shot of your people. They were forcing them to take Nicolae's mark."

"Did they take it?" Ty said.

"A few did. Some didn't, and they were killed."

NINE

Flight to Petra

JUDD sat in the tiny car near a runway on the outskirts of Saarbrücken and listened to Jacques explain the history of the region. The area had switched hands so many times in the past century that it was hard to keep up with all the changes. But one thing was certain: The Global Community now controlled Saarbrücken.

The city had changed drastically after the wrath of the Lamb earthquake. Buildings that were hundreds of years old had toppled, and much of the city had been left in rubble. Miraculously, a few church buildings had survived. When the Global Community arrived to rebuild, the churches were replaced with worship centers for Nicolae Carpathia. One church's spire had fallen, and in its place was a statue of Nicolae that everyone was required to worship three times each day.

Jacques parked behind a grove of narrow trees and pulled out binoculars. A gentle rain had begun to fall. Soon it turned into a downpour.

Five hours later the four remained in the car waiting for word from the pilot and rubbing the inside of the windshield trying to see outside.

"I don't think the flight is coming," Jacques said.

Westin shifted in his seat. "They would have called. They know they're leaving us vulnerable here."

"How are we supposed to get to the runway with all those GC officers down there?" Lionel said. "We can't just walk through them."

Judd kept calling Chang and finally reached him in New Babylon. "All I can tell you is that the flight should have been there five hours ago," Chang said. "The GC in Saarbrücken have been told this flight has sensitive materials in part of the cargo hold. They're supposed to load the supplies as quickly as they can and let the plane get airborne."

"If it does get here, how do we get on?" Judd said.

"When the plane lands, you guys will move as close to the end of the runway as you can. When it taxis to the end and the coast is clear, the pilot will flash a light in the cockpit. You might have to climb a fence, but the pilot will stop and make sure you get on before he leaves."

Judd thought of Taylor Graham, a pilot who had taken a lot of chances to help the kids. It was a plan Taylor would have loved, but Judd felt queasy as he explained it to the others.

"If we stay much longer," Jacques said, "someone may spot us."

"Where else can we go?" Westin said.

"I have relatives nearby, but I don't know their stance on the Global Community."

"I'd rather risk staying here than run into a nest of Carpathia followers who will turn us in," Westin said.

The rain continued and a dense fog moved into the area. Judd rolled down his window slightly and heard the drone of an airplane in the distance. His phone chirped and Judd grabbed it.

"There was some kind of delay at the last location," Chang said. "The pilot couldn't get in touch because he was in the middle of a bunch of Peacekeepers. He says the fog may help you guys. Move to the runway and wait for his signal."

Judd relayed the message and looked at Jacques. "I can't tell you how much we appreciate—"

Jacques held up a hand and smiled. "No need to thank me. You would have done the same. We will pray for your safe return." He looked at Westin. "And we will pray for your safety flying for the Tribulation Force. It should be quite different from your work with Z-Van."

Westin put a hand on the man's shoulder. "Your son died in my place. I'll never forget him or what you've done. If you ever need help, call."

Judd, Westin, and Lionel quickly moved from the car toward the end of the runway. Judd stuffed his phone in his jacket and shielded his face from the driving rain. They found the fence and ran around the perimeter until they were at the end of the runway. The fog was so thick that Judd couldn't see the airport terminal or the plane. He wondered if they would be able to see the pilot's signal.

The three hunkered down in the tall grass and tried to stay dry. Judd squinted into the mist. The last fence was at least twelve feet high and had razor wire around the top.

"Let's see if there's another way instead of going over it," Westin said.

They scaled the first two fences, and Lionel's sweater caught on a barb and tore as he went over.

When they reached the third fence, Westin crab-walked along the chain-link structure, pulling at the bottom. It was buried, but they had no idea how far. "We can't go over without getting cut, and it looks like we'll have to do some digging to get under."

"No wire cutters?" Lionel said.

Westin shook his head. Lionel pulled out his pocketknife, but Westin told him to put it away. "That'll never cut through that wire."

Lionel found a soft spot in the ground and began to dig with his hands. After a few minutes and a lot of mud, Judd and Lionel had reached the bottom of the fence and started yanking it up from the ground.

Judd's phone chirped, and he fished it out with dirty hands.

"Yeah, we're all loaded and set for takeoff," a man said in an official tone. "I'm going to take one last ride down the runway if you're okay with that."

"We'll be waiting for you," Judd said.

"That's a roger."

The phone clicked, and Judd, Lionel, and

Westin worked frantically to dig out a hole large enough to crawl through. Westin stood and pulled at the fence with all his might. First Judd, then Lionel squeezed under the muddy area. Lionel and Judd pushed at the fence from the other side until Westin made it through.

The engines were deafening as the plane roared toward them. Judd's first instinct was to hold back in case the pilot couldn't see them through the fog, but Westin raced forward to the runway.

Lionel saw the plane first and pointed. It was a hundred yards away and closing in fast. Something flashed in the cockpit, and Westin bolted for the rear of the aircraft. Judd gasped when he saw the GC insignia on the side but kept moving.

The plane stopped, a door in the rear opened slightly, and Judd reached for a hand sticking out. He nearly let go and fell back when he saw the mark of Nicolae Carpathia on the pilot's forehead.

Vicki awoke from a nap and sat up on her cot. She and four other girls had a cabin to themselves. It wasn't as nice as Colin's house or even the schoolhouse, but she felt safe.

She found the others eating in the main cabin and located Zeke. The man hadn't changed much since she had first met him. He still wore his hair long and had tattoos on his flabby arms, but there was something different, a softness about him she didn't remember. Zeke had been into booze and drugs before God had changed his life. His mother and two sisters had died in a fire the night of the disappearances. Vicki guessed all the changes of the past few years had really affected him.

"I guess you heard about my dad," Zeke said.

Vicki told him what she had learned from Natalie Bishop, who had witnessed Zeke's father's execution.

Zeke nearly broke down. "I never thought I'd hear anything about what actually happened. I knew Dad would never come out of that GC lockup alive."

Zeke told Vicki about his experiences with the Tribulation Force at the Strong Building in Chicago. "Buck Williams came to get me. I've been able to help people with their disguises and new clothes and such. You should see what I did to Dr. Rosenzweig."

When Vicki brought up Kenny Williams,

Zeke's eyes misted. "I'm gonna miss that little fella. You know there's nothing like a kid to help change your perspective. Things would be so stressful and then that little guy came in and the whole room changed."

Vicki noticed Cheryl Tifanne in the corner. In the short time Cheryl had been gone, her stomach had grown. "You know Cheryl is expecting a baby."

Zeke nodded. "I heard all about it from Tom Fogarty. Sure was something the way you hooked those people up."

Zeke was silent for a moment, then turned to Vicki. "Remember when you came to the gas station to get a makeover? What was the guy's name you were always fighting with?"

"Judd?"

Zeke smiled. "Yeah, whatever happened to him?"

Vicki told Zeke everything, from the arguments between her and Judd to his recent phone calls.

"Sounds like your friend has done some growing up," Zeke said.

"So have I."

"If I can help get him back here, let me know."

Judd jumped into the plane and looked around for other Peacekeepers, but there were none. Lionel and Westin climbed in and seemed equally shocked that the pilot had the mark of Carpathia.

"Oh, this," the pilot said, rolling his eyes and reaching for his forehead. "I forgot I still had it on."

The man was just under six feet tall, had sandy blond hair, and a day's growth of beard. On his forehead was a -6, the mark of the United North American States. He put his palm to the mark, rubbed it hard, then grasped the edges with his fingers and peeled it from his skin. "Friend of mine made this for me. Lets me move around the GC without drawing suspicion." He put out his hand. "Jerry Kingston. Are you Westin?"

"Yeah."

"Then you can help me get this bird in the—"

The radio squawked in the front.

"That's the tower. They'll want to know why I'm sitting on the end of the runway."

"I'm surprised they could see you in this fog," Judd said.

Jerry motioned to a row of seats. "You guys

get buckled in. We retrofitted this one to give us only a few seats and lots of cargo space."

Jerry spoke to the tower in German, and Judd asked what he had said. "I told them I'd stopped because I thought I saw some kind of animal burrowing under the fence at the end of the runway. Told them to send someone to check it out as fast as possible."

When they were safely in the air, Jerry patted Westin on the shoulder and said he was taking a break. He snatched three sodas from a small refrigerator and gave one to Judd and Lionel. "Sorry I was late. Had some engine trouble and couldn't break free from the GC long enough to signal you guys. How'd you get stranded way out here?"

Judd quickly told Jerry their story. The man raised his eyebrows when he found out that Judd had met Chang Wong in New Babylon. "Chang is our lifeline out here. Without him working his computer magic and making the GC think we're legit, we wouldn't have any supplies moving around and I'd be dead."

"How did you get involved with the Tribulation Force?" Lionel said.

Jerry sat back and put his hands behind his head. "Every time I tell this, it's almost too unbelievable."

"Try us," Lionel said.

"I've been a military guy all my life. Attended the Air Force Academy. I was doing a tour overseas when the disappearances happened. A friend of mine and I were on a routine flight, talking back and forth. Brad had a family back home. I was single. He never went out drinking. I couldn't stop. You get the picture.

"Brad talked a lot about spiritual stuff, you know, asking me what I thought would happen after I died, if there was a heaven, those kinds of things. He was religious, but you wouldn't have found a better friend.

"Anyway, we're talking, going about five hundred miles an hour. Brad was in his plane, me in mine, and I did a flip and flew upside down just over his cockpit. He laughed, called me a hot dog, and later did the same thing. He pulled over the top of me and stayed there. I was close enough to see the smile on the guy's face.

"He starts a sentence and all of sudden cuts out. I look up and his helmet is rolling around inside the canopy, his shoes too. His flight suit is buckled in, just hanging there, but the guy is gone. I mean absolutely nowhere."

"What did you think at that moment?" Judd said.

"First thing I thought was I needed to get out of his way. If there's nobody at the controls and you're that close together, it's trouble. I pulled away and tried to figure it out. His plane went into a spin and crashed. They found the wreckage but no body. I could have told them they weren't going to find one."

"Did that make you want to know about God?" Lionel said.

"Nope. I went about as far away from God as you can get after that. I tried all kinds of stuff. When the Global Community came on the scene, I was glad to join and they stationed me in Europe.

"Then I started noticing things about the GC. Orders that came down that didn't seem like what a peace-loving group would do. When I challenged them, I was told the orders came from the highest level."

"What did they ask you to do?" Judd said.

"Just drop a little nuclear warhead on London," Jerry said with a scowl. "Can you believe I did that?"

"I remember that," Lionel said. "Thousands were killed."

"Hundreds of thousands. Carpathia told us it was for the good of the Global Community, that more people would live because of our actions. I couldn't live with myself, so I decided to end it. I was going to fly my jet into the ocean, me in it."

"What happened?" Judd said.

"I flew out there, but something Brad said clicked. He had talked about life after death a lot and said he was sure where he was going. That stuck with me, and I had to admit I didn't know where I was going after I hit the water. I was headed in a nosedive and pulled out just in time. When I got back to the base, I did a search on the Web for the word *eternity*. Guess where I wound up?"

"Tsion Ben-Judah?" Lionel said.

"Bingo! I prayed the prayer and everything changed."

"Did you stay in the GC?"

Jerry shook his head. "I know some believers can work for the GC and I admire them, but I couldn't think of dropping another bomb. I actually took my plane, one of the newest the GC had at the time, and crashed it near the Atlantic. Of course, I got out of the thing, but they listed me as a casualty. I made my way to a Co-op location and volunteered. Been flying ever since."

Judd was astounded at the places and things Jerry had seen and done.

"I've never been to Petra, though," Jerry said. "This should be something!"

TEN

Walking in Petra

TOUCHING down near Petra was a thrill Judd never dreamed he would have. Flying over the city carved out of rock was breathtaking. But seeing a million people in and around the area, along with the pool of water that bubbled up on the floor of the desert, was amazing. A caravan of people met the plane to help unload supplies. Though people who lived in Petra asked Westin and Jerry to stay, they refueled and got back in the plane.

Westin turned and stuck out a hand to Judd. "I can't thank you enough for what you've done for me." His chin quivered. "I'll see you somewhere down the road."

"We'll look forward to it," Judd said.

As Westin's plane flew away, a familiar voice yelled behind Judd. It was Sam

Goldberg, who was so excited he hardly seemed to touch the ground as he ran.

Sam led Judd and Lionel through the narrow passage called a Siq and showed them the computer center.

Mr. Stein threw up his hands when he saw Judd and Lionel and hugged them tightly. "I didn't know if we would ever be together again," he said. "Tell me everything."

Judd and Lionel took turns telling their story. When they were through, Mr. Stein joined hands with them. "Our Father, we praise your name today for the protection you have given our two brothers. You have done mighty things through them, and I pray you would do even more before the return of your Son."

As Mr. Stein prayed, Judd heard the flutter of wings above them. Birds landed in small groups around the city.

"And we thank you once again for your marvelous provision."

Sam picked up a quail and held it out to Judd. "Ready for dinner?"

Lionel couldn't get over the taste of the wafers that appeared on the ground each morning in Petra. He wanted to take a sample back to his friends in the States but knew the sweet-tasting food would spoil. The wafer tasted heavenly, and the mix of quail and manna was the perfect evening meal.

For the next few days, Lionel wandered through the camps, talking with new believers and listening to stories of miracles God had performed. Many spoke in different languages, but Lionel understood them all.

Some did not have the mark of the believer, and Lionel couldn't believe these people could see God's deliverance and not give their lives to him. He talked with Judd, Sam, and Mr. Stein, but no one could explain why these people still rejected God.

The answer came one evening as Naomi interrupted Sam's interview of Judd and Lionel for his Petra Diaries. "Dr. Ben-Judah and Micah would like to speak with you."

Lionel and Judd followed Naomi up the hill to a cave entrance. Inside was a small meeting room used by a group of elders, one of whom was Naomi's father.

Tsion Ben-Judah greeted the two like they were long-lost members of his family. He introduced everyone and had them sit. "I met these young men when I first became a member of the Tribulation Force," Tsion explained to the others. "And how are your friends in the Young Trib Force?"

Judd and Lionel told him what they knew about Vicki and the others. Tsion hadn't heard about the close call with the Global Community and the destruction of Colin Dial's house in Wisconsin.

"I am afraid we have some very difficult days ahead," Tsion said. "The first three and a half years of the Tribulation were terrible, the worst the world has ever seen. The last three and a half years . . ." The man's voice trailed off.

"Something's bothering me," Lionel said.

Tsion motioned for him to continue, so Lionel asked why people who had seen God's miracles still didn't believe.

Tsion sighed. "It bothers me as well, and it is why we daily give the message. Every time Micah and I speak, we make sure we include the gospel with the teaching for the day. Sometimes only one or two respond, but we will continue to preach."

"What's keeping them from the truth?" Lionel said.

Tsion scooted closer. "It is not our responsibility to save people. That is God's job. We must be faithful to give the message."

"But couldn't God simply make them believe?"

"Our God is sovereign, which means he is involved in all of the events of this world. He

knew you would ask this question. He knew
Judd would not accept his parents' faith and
be left behind. He knew my family would be
killed."

"Why didn't he stop that?" Lionel said.

"Our ways are not his ways. I do not
understand why he let my family be killed,
but I know that he is in control. And though
we would like to make everyone believe the
truth about him, he has chosen to give each
person the freedom to choose or reject him."

"Doesn't it say somewhere in the Bible that
God wants everyone to believe?"

Tsion nodded. "In Second Peter we read
that 'He does not want anyone to perish.' He
wants everyone to be sorry for their sins and
turn to him for forgiveness. It is our privilege
to prayerfully explain the gospel and let God
work on hearts to convince people they need
to accept Jesus as Savior and Lord."

Lionel scrunched up his face and looked
around the room. "I'm not trying to be difficult. I really don't understand how God can
want people to come to him and not make it
happen."

"If God forced people to become believers,
they would have no choice. They would be
acting like robots. Instead, God demon-
strated his love by dying for them, in their

place on the cross, and allows each person to accept or reject God's sacrifice."

Micah leaned forward. "I would love to take everyone without the mark of the believer and force them to faith. It would be the best thing for them. But God wants us to pray, be faithful in giving the message, and explain clearly who Jesus is. The responsibility of choice is theirs."

Tsion added, "Never underestimate the power of God in convicting the people you have shared with. Keep praying for them and warn them not to take the mark of the beast."

Over the next few days, Vicki and the others settled into their new home in Avery, Wisconsin. Vicki could tell Becky was having a hard time with their living conditions. Some of the cabins were more modern, while others had no electricity or running water.

Tanya grieved the death of her father. Vicki tried to comfort her, but the girl was overcome with guilt. "If I hadn't left the cave, none of this would have happened. All of those people would still be alive."

Her brother, Ty, joined Vicki. "If you hadn't gone to see Vicki, we wouldn't be believers now. Dad made his choice, and I'm sad he made the wrong one, but it was his choice."

"Why couldn't God have changed his heart?" Tanya sobbed. "We'll never see him again, don't you understand?"

Vicki sat with her and silently prayed. When Tanya fell asleep, Vicki went to the main cabin to check on the others. Marshall Jameson and Zeke had recently brought the computers up to date. The laptop Vicki brought was a welcome addition, and Mark had found several new items of information on-line.

Vicki felt strange around Mark now, but she tried not to let it affect her. He had been the one who insisted she leave, and now they were together again. If Mark had a problem with it, Vicki couldn't tell.

Each morning someone from the group would lead in teaching. Most of the time, Marshall Jameson read from Tsion Ben-Judah's Web site or expanded on the man's teaching. To her surprise, Zeke was asked to lead a few sessions. At first Zeke seemed reluctant, but the more he led the Bible studies, the better he got and the more he seemed to enjoy it.

"As we get settled in," Zeke said one morning, "I think God's gonna make it clear what he wants us to do. He hasn't left us here just to crawl in a hole. I don't know about the rest of you, but I'm hoping we're able to bring new believers here. We have the room, and if we fix up some of the run-down cabins, we could bring in a lot more."

Zeke told the group about a situation that had happened at the Strong Building in Chicago before the Tribulation Force had to scatter. Chloe had discovered hidden believers in a Chicago building. "Chloe got chewed out, but we're glad she found 'em. That bomb would have wiped out those people."

In the evenings, everyone met and Marshall Jameson asked a different person to tell how God had changed them. Vicki was thrilled to hear the stories of her friends, as well as those she didn't know well. Thomas Fogarty could hardly contain his emotion when he told his story.

Then one night, Marshall himself took the floor. "Some of you know my story, but for those who are new, I'm one of the people who shouldn't be here. I was the owner of a Christian radio station."

Vicki's eyes widened, and a hush fell over the room.

Marshall looked at the floor and shook his head. "I heard every preacher in the country, every sermon, could quote Bible verses in my sleep, but when the Rapture happened, I found out I didn't have Christ.

"My mom and dad took me to church when I was young, but it was a social thing. My friends were there. My dad offered to pay my way to a Christian college, so I took him up on it. Studied business because I wanted to make a lot of money. A big change came when I walked into the campus radio station. A friend of mine let me read the news late one night, and I was hooked. I switched to communications and couldn't get enough of radio.

"My parents died in a plane crash when I was in my twenties. The will divided the money equally among us three kids—I have an older sister and younger brother—and I took my share and bought a little radio station.

"That investment paid off. I had Christian ministries coming to me and buying airtime. I hired professionals and even had an article about me in one of the radio magazines. Our ratings were going higher, I raised our fees, and still people were willing to pay. I was making money, doing a show every day, and living a dream.

"I had a wife and two little boys. She was the one who saw the truth and confronted me. She accused me of living a double life. I was going to churches and asking people to listen, but she knew I was just in it for the money." Marshall ran a hand through his hair. "I could talk about God, I could pray in front of people, I could put on a show on the radio, but I had no relationship with God."

Vicki leaned forward. "What happened on the night of the disappearances?"

"I got a call from my overnight guy, wiry fellow, always wore jeans and ate corned beef sandwiches at night. The morning people always complained about him. Anyway, Jack called in sick. Our backup guy was on vacation, and I'd just had a fight with my wife, so I went over and relieved him.

"We used a satellite feed during the overnight, so all I had to do was make sure the right buttons were pushed and the volume controls were set. The guy on the show that night was live, taking calls, playing music, and telling stories. He was right in the middle of a story about some things he and his wife had gone through. They had fought, hurt each other, and been driven apart. Well, I was interested. I sat up and listened when he said their marriage had come alive.

"The phone rang, but I turned up the volume. It kept ringing, so I answered and heard my wife's voice. She was awake and saw I wasn't there and thought I might have gone to the station. She wanted to talk. I told her I would call her back and hung up.

"The guy was right at the point where things had changed between him and his wife when his voice cut out. I had the speakers up really loud, and I heard his last word, then a clunk, like his headphones had fallen to the table. I thought the guy had a heart attack. There was silence. Nothing.

"I called the network studio, and the phone rang and rang. Alarms and buzzers blared near the transmitter, so I pulled up a song and started it. While it was playing, the phone rang again. I thought it was my wife, but instead there was a woman who'd been listening to the station with a friend. They were delivering newspapers, and the woman riding with her disappeared. Then she said, 'Do you think this was the Rapture?'

"That's when it clicked. I'd heard about the Rapture from the time I was a kid, but I never thought it would happen to me. I called my wife. No answer. I called everybody on the station payroll, but the only person who answered was an advertising executive. We'd been left behind."

"What did you do?" Vicki said.

"I put on about an hour's worth of music

and went looking for a program I'd shoved in the back of my desk. A local preacher sent out a recording to every station about the end times. I thought the guy was a kook to waste his money like that, but I kept it to pull out and have a laugh. I listened to the whole thing and prayed the prayer at the end, asking God to forgive me and show me what he wanted me to do."

"What happened to the station?"

"I played as many Christian programs as possible and tried to help people see the truth. When the Global Community came to power, they shut us down. They were coming to take me to a reeducation camp when I made my way here."

Vicki imagined what it was like for Marshall to discover his wife and children gone. Many of the old feelings of regret washed over her as he finished his story.

That night, Vicki cried, remembering her parents, her sister, and her brother. But one thought kept coming back: *Just like Marshall, I'll see my family again.*

ELEVEN

Charlie's Notebook

EACH day Judd awoke with a new sense of God's provision and a fresh yearning for home. Their flight from Petra to South Carolina had been delayed by Global Community activity, but Judd kept in contact with Chang Wong for updates.

Judd was glad for a few days of safety without having to worry about a GC attack. He struck up a friendship with the computer whiz, Naomi, and met more of Sam's friends. Judd and Lionel helped people build tents and shelters, and in their spare time they climbed the heights of Petra and explored the ancient ruins with Sam.

One night Judd e-mailed Chang about the upcoming flight and got a call an hour later. Chang seemed upset.

"I spoke with my sister, Ming. My father is dead."

"What?"

"Ming met with a local villager in China who knew my mom and dad. My father never took the mark, and the villager said he died with honor."

"He became a believer?"

"Yes. And my mother is living about fifty miles from there in the mountains. Ming may be visiting her now."

"I'm sorry for your loss, but I'm excited that your father finally came to the truth."

"Yes. I can't help but think that he's watching me now and that he's proud of what I'm doing."

Chang told Judd that the flight back to the States had been delayed again and there was a chance that Westin Jakes might fly them. "He fits in well."

Judd asked how things were going in the States. Chang said he had been having trouble getting into the computer files of some of the United North American States officials. "This Commander Fulcire has me worried. The code name for the new program they've started is *BoHu*, but I can't find out what it is."

"Sounds like an African rice dish," Judd joked.

Chang was silent for a moment and Judd apologized. He realized it had been a long time since he had felt free enough to laugh or

make a joke. Chang said he would get back
with more details on Judd's flight.

The next day Global Community News
Network showed chilling scenes of people
without Carpathia's mark being rounded up.
Even more sinister was the video of young
Jewish men and women who were loaded
into GC trucks for transport to concentration
camps.

People who did not worship Nicolae
Carpathia three times each day were beaten
in the streets, though Judd wondered how
the GC knew who hadn't worshiped that day.
Morale Monitors with clubs and electric
prods moved through lines of worshipers
who seemed tired of kneeling and praying to
Nicolae's statue.

The documentary by Lars Rahlmost finally
ran on international television the following
night. With the voices of famous actors,
actresses, and musicians, including Z-Van, the
film chronicled Carpathia's resurrection and
the reaction of people throughout the world.

Before the documentary played, Lars
appeared in an interview. "Most people
would take at least a year and perhaps two
to put together what we have done in only
weeks. But we've come out with this special
film for two reasons. We want to praise the

one who deserves all praise and to convince those who are putting their lives in jeopardy by not taking the mark. Our goal is to help people see the truth that Nicolae is not to be feared, but loved and served, as he loves and serves us."

Lars ended his interview by kneeling in his living room in front of a statue of Nicolae that had been signed by the potentate. The man closed his eyes and kissed the statue's hand.

Hundreds of thousands watching in Petra booed and hissed, but a few seemed swayed by the opening of the film that Nicolae might be God.

The resurrection of Nicolae was played out dramatically, and Judd recalled the horror of actually being in New Babylon during the event. Musicians, poets, actors, and politicians from around the world paid tribute to the man. Then came interviews with people who had bought Nicolae's lie. The saddest, Judd thought, were the children who sang songs and recited poems in the man's honor.

One rosy-cheeked young girl, no older than three, sang a song that churned Judd's stomach.

> "Nicolae loves me, this I see.
> He came back from the dead for me.

Little ones praise him in song.
They are weak, but he is strong.
Yes, Nicolae loves me.
Yes, Nicolae loves me.
Yes, Nicolae loves me; he came back from
   the dead."

When the documentary was over, the lights went out on the screen and a lone figure stood high above on a cliff. Micah raised both hands. "Friends, we debated whether or not to show you this documentary tonight, but in the end we believe that truth is stronger than the fiction you have just witnessed. Do not be swayed by this dragon. Many years ago Jesus said of him, 'He was a murderer from the beginning and has always hated the truth. There is no truth in him. When he lies, it is consistent with his character; for he is a liar and the father of lies.'

"Whom would you rather follow, the man who laid down his life as a ransom for you or the one who says you must worship his statue or be killed?"

"How do you explain Nicolae's resurrection?" someone yelled from the front. "How could he do that if he were not God?"

"Jesus said, 'I am the resurrection and the

life. Those who believe in me, even though they die like everyone else, will live again. They are given eternal life for believing in me and will never perish.'"

"But how do we know?" someone whined from behind Judd.

Micah continued preaching, trying to persuade those who had not yet chosen.

Judd heard someone behind him say, "I'm not choosing. I believe Nicolae is a murderer, but I can't believe in Jesus either."

"Do not think that you can remain neutral about this issue," Micah continued. "Jesus himself said, 'Anyone who isn't helping me opposes me, and anyone who isn't working with me is actually working against me.' If you choose against Christ, you are choosing *for* Nicolae."

Conversations lasted into the night. Judd wondered what the documentary had done to people around the world. Was it making them want to take Carpathia's mark?

Vicki had brought the laptop and only a few things she could fit into an old duffel bag. As she neared the bottom of the bag, she found Charlie's notebook Becky had given her.

Vicki had thought about reading it but

now was glad she hadn't. She found Charlie playing with Phoenix in one of the cabins and handed it to him.

"My writing book," Charlie said, his eyes wide. "Where did you find it?"

Vicki explained he had left it at Colin's house, and Charlie hugged the book like it was a long-lost friend. "Did you read it?"

Vicki shook her head.

"'Cause I write stuff in here that I don't want anybody to see," Charlie continued. "I even wrote stuff about you."

"Me?"

"Uh-huh. Want to know what I said?"

Vicki smiled, thinking Charlie had written about their adventures. "Sure. What did you put down?"

Charlie opened the spiral notebook and flipped through the pages. He found the right page and folded the book open. "You know when they have a wedding and the man stands up there and says stuff?"

"You mean the preacher?"

"Yeah. Well, I wrote down a bunch of verses I think they ought to read at your wedding."

Vicki's mouth dropped open. "What makes you think I'm going to be married?"

"I just know it. You and Judd are going to

get married. Other people think that, but they don't talk much about it."

"Like who?"

"I don't know . . . Shelly, Becky, and some of the others."

Vicki reached for the notebook and saw Charlie's scrawled handwriting. His letters had gotten smaller—he used only two lines to write a sentence—but she had to study each word to make it out.

Charlie had written out the entire passage of First Corinthians 13. He had also found other verses in the Bible that talked about a love between a husband and wife.

The one that caught her attention was from the Song of Solomon. "For love is as strong as death. . . . Love flashes like fire, the brightest kind of flame. Many waters cannot quench love; neither can rivers drown it."

Charlie blushed. "Do you think I could read this at your wedding?"

Vicki closed the notebook and handed it back to Charlie. "If I ever get married, I want you to be there and read those. But I honestly don't know if Judd and I are going to get married."

Charlie smiled. "I'm willing to wait and see."

Judd had been thrilled to speak with Tsion Ben-Judah, but he was equally excited a few days later when he found Rayford Steele, a pilot and one of the original Tribulation Force members. They met outside the computer building, and Rayford invited Judd back to his small place. Captain Steele's house, if it could be called that, was a tiny but well-built building that was big enough for a bed and his computer equipment.

Two glass jars sat near the computer. One was filled with water, the other manna. On Rayford's screen was a picture of a toddler Judd guessed to be about two years old. The boy smiled and leaned toward the camera. In the background was Chloe Williams, Rayford's daughter.

"That's Kenny," Rayford said, chuckling. "He calls me 'Gampa.'" Judd noticed tears in the man's eyes. "I miss seeing that little guy more than anything. I can't wait to get back to San Diego."

"Why haven't you gone back?"

Rayford sighed. "Everybody has had to be flexible since moving out of Chicago. I'm able to keep track of things from here, even though my heart's in California. I'll get back there one day."

The two talked about all that had happened to them in the past three and a half years. Judd told Rayford his plan to get back to the States. They relived the deaths of Bruce Barnes, Ryan Daley, and others, including Rayford's second wife, Amanda. "Sometimes I wish we'd never met."

"You regret getting married during the Tribulation?"

"No, I just meant that if Amanda hadn't met me, she wouldn't have been on the plane that went down. I don't regret one minute of our time together. I wish she were here now to see Petra."

Rayford put a hand on Judd's shoulder and prayed for him. Judd picked up the prayer and asked God to help Rayford get back to his family.

A few days later the call Judd had awaited came from Chang. "I've worked with Chloe Steele. Looks like you're finally going home."

When the plane touched down on the runway near Petra three days later, Lionel and Judd were waiting. Sam Goldberg and Mr. Stein prayed with them, and they all embraced. Sam told Judd to make sure he communicated with them during their trip.

Judd watched the rocks of Petra fade on

the horizon. The sun glinted through the window, and he shaded his eyes. He stuffed the directions for their meeting in South Carolina into a pocket and sat back.

I'm finally going home, Judd thought.

TWELVE

Mr. Whalum

LIONEL was excited when he discovered their pilot was a black man whose first name was the same as his. Lionel Whalum was a compact man, with glasses and salt-and-pepper hair. At first he seemed disinterested in Judd and Lionel, but that changed once they were in the air. He motioned them to the cockpit, and they approached and introduced themselves.

"Mr. Whalum is fine," the man said as he gave them both a firm handshake. "You start calling me Lionel and both of us will come running." He had a laugh that started in his toes and worked its way up through his body. "What brought you two to Petra?"

Judd began their story, and Mr. Whalum locked eyes with him. When Judd told him about helping Z-Van, meeting Westin, and

Perryn's death, Mr. Whalum shook his head. "I saw coverage of that on TV. I'm sorry. You two have been away a long time."

Judd nodded. "You giving us a flight back to the States is an answer to prayer."

Mr. Whalum smiled. "I've seen a few of those in the past three and a half years." He explained how he had become involved in the Co-op, flying deliveries all around the world. His latest trip to Petra had brought more of the ready-made buildings like the one Rayford Steele used.

"How'd you get involved in the Co-op?" Judd said.

"I got hooked up with them through a couple of people. Chang Wong switched my information on the GC database, and I was good to go. I was able to use my contacts to deliver materials."

Mr. Whalum told them he was from Long Grove, Illinois. He and his wife and three kids had moved from Chicago to the northern suburb after financial success.

"How did you become a believer?" Lionel said.

"I love telling that story," Mr. Whalum said. "You know, there's nothing wrong with success, but I think that was part of why I was left behind. *Things* became really important to me. Getting a bigger house, more money. It was a trap that kept me working harder and forgetting what's really important.

"And get this, my wife and I were church people. Good people. But I always thought my family was a little too emotional about the whole church thing. When Felicia and I got married, we didn't go much, and when we did, it was to a 'higher' church where people didn't get all emotional. My family would have said it was dead."

Lionel smiled, remembering that his mother had said the exact same thing when his family had visited another church.

"We wanted something that didn't have the jumpy music and loud voices, and we found it after we moved. Nobody preached that we were sinners or needed to get right with God.

"But our kids—two girls with a boy in between—went off to college and wound up in the same kind of church I grew up in. They wrote and begged us to get saved."

"Must have shocked you," Judd said.

"You bet. But it didn't change me. Then a really successful man in our neighborhood invited Felicia and me to a Bible study. This guy had made it big, but he talked about God and Jesus like it was natural. We read the Bible and discussed it. Simple.

"We kept going until one night the guy got us alone and laid out how to become a born-again Christian. I'd heard it all before. I knew what he was going to say. So I said I appreciated his concern and asked if he would pray for us. Instead of just saying he would, he did right there."

"But you didn't pray," Lionel said.

Mr. Whalum shook his head. "And two days later, millions of people disappeared, including every last person in that Bible study except us. And all three of our kids were gone."

"When did you pray for God to forgive you?" Lionel said.

"Right then. Didn't take us ten minutes after we found out about what had happened to know we'd missed the boat, so to speak. Now we're doing all we can through the Co-op to help believers, tell as many unbelievers the truth, and even take a few people into our home."

Vicki rushed to the main cabin behind Shelly to see the message from Sam. Vicki burst into the room, and others near the computer moved.

Judd and Lionel wanted me to tell you they are

on their way home! Sam wrote. *I think you'll find the advance copy of my Petra Diaries to be very interesting.*

Vicki printed the document and hurried to her cabin clutching the pages. She tried not to show her excitement, but everyone snickered as she ran from the building.

She lay on her cot and spread the pages out. Sam's letter was an interview with the two, and she drank in every word. Though the boy's writing was simple, his questions were good, and Vicki learned more about the danger Judd and Lionel had encountered.

She finished the pages and leaned back on her pillow. *If Judd and Lionel get into South Carolina tomorrow morning, it'll take at least a few days to work their way north.* Vicki turned a page over, drew seven boxes, and checked one of them. *Judd's going to be here in a week!*

The plane touched down at an old military base on an island in South Carolina. The Global Community still used part of the base, but Chang had worked his magic and planted information that the GC were training a new pilot and needed a test landing.

Judd and Lionel said good-bye to Mr. Whalum and thanked him.

"You guys stay safe," Mr. Whalum said. "Wish I could have taken you to Wisconsin, but I'm supposed to pick up some critical supplies further up the coast. Let me know if I can help you."

The two slipped into the trees surrounding the runway and watched the plane take off again. They stayed hidden for a few minutes, listening for any movement. Lionel coughed and grabbed at his throat. "Must have picked up something on the flight over here. My throat's all scratchy."

Judd had always like the heat and humidity of the low country. He wished he could bottle the smell of the salt water and take it with him. He closed his eyes and took a deep breath.

"Smells like fish," Lionel whispered.

"Yeah, isn't it great?"

"I guess, if you like fish."

Judd found an overgrown path and a series of frayed ropes, old tires, and other obstacles. He pointed to a platform that had been built on a tree limb and several boards leading up. "After you."

Once they had climbed to the platform, Judd pulled out binoculars and focused on the main base in the distance. A Global Community flag flew high above the building. In the distance Judd saw the lights of a small town.

"Where are Tom and Luke?" Lionel said. "I feel like a target waiting to get shot at."

"I don't like it any more than you do, but they said they'd meet us at the fort."

Judd got his bearings, climbed down, and led them to the water. They would need to cross a deep river to reach their friends, and Judd quickly found the hidden rowboat in a clump of brush. Because there was a slack tide, the water wasn't as choppy, but Judd found the rowing difficult and tiring.

Two hours later they pushed the boat onto a sandy beach and ran inland over mounds of sun-bleached oyster shells.

"That's the marsh grass Tom warned me about," Judd said, pointing. "We go in that and we're up to our knees in mud."

"Why didn't Tom and Luke come get us?" Lionel said.

"Less dangerous if we meet them, I guess. We'll go to their hideout after we meet them at the fort."

Judd checked his compass, and they moved west, looking at the map and directions Tom and Luke Gowin had given.

Lionel pulled out a plastic bag from his pocket, and Judd recognized the smashed

manna. The sight made Judd's mouth water.
Going back to regular food would be difficult
after the refreshing quail, manna, and water
of Petra.

Lionel pulled out the sweet, breadlike food
and frowned. "Just like I figured, it's spoiled.
I wanted to show this to the others."

"I wish we could all stay in Petra," Judd
said, walking through the sea grass on the
dunes. "Food, water, God's protection,
fellowship every day, and about a million
other believers."

"You don't want to be here, with all this
fishy smell?" Lionel said with a smile.

"My dad used to say that there was no
better place on earth than in God's will. I
wish I would have listened to him. But it's
not too late to live that. Evidently God wants
us out in the world reaching other people
with the message until he returns."

"I know who you want to reach." Lionel
smirked. "And I've got a feeling we're not
going to stop until we get to Wisconsin."

Judd grinned and shook his head. "Lay off
the Vicki stuff, okay? I don't even know if
she'll want me back."

"The way you've changed? Man, she'll be
dancing better than those people in Petra
when she sees you."

"What do you mean, changed?"

Lionel cleared his throat and unzipped his backpack, looking for a water bottle. He found it and took a long drink. "You don't think I've noticed? Not your looks." Lionel tapped Judd's chest. "In there. Something's been going on. You're treating people differently. I mean, you're not perfect, but you've improved."

Judd spotted the ruins of an old fort in the distance. They crept up to it, hoping to find Luke and Tom inside, but it was deserted. They sat with their backs to an inner wall and rested.

"So what happened to you?" Lionel said. "How'd you change so much?"

"I've been working on listening to others. There's even a verse I found. . . ."

"Which one?"

"It's in Philippians 2." Judd closed his eyes and put his head back against the stone wall. 'Don't be selfish; don't live to make a good impression on others. Be humble, thinking of others as better than yourself. Don't think only about your own affairs, but be interested in others, too, and what they are doing.'"

Lionel smiled. "That's it. I can tell you haven't just memorized it, you've really tried to pract—"

Judd sat up quickly and held up a hand when he heard movement outside. Two people walked toward them through the brush a hundred yards away. Both wore regular clothes, not GC uniforms, but Judd didn't know if they were Luke and Tom.

Judd and Lionel gathered their things quietly and watched from inside the fort. Lionel wanted to walk toward them, but Judd snagged his arm.

"They're walking straight this way," Lionel said. "It has to be them."

"Just stay out of sight a little longer."

"So much for the compliment I gave you."

The two headed straight for the fort, but Judd wondered if they were simply following the worn path. *Would Luke and Tom walk out in the open like that?* Two minutes went by before they heard men's voices.

"Those guys are talking like they own this place," Judd whispered. "Tom and Luke wouldn't do that." He stood and looked over the crumbling wall. The approaching men went down a dip in the path so Judd could only see their heads. One had sandy-colored hair, the other a darker brown. *It could be Tom and Luke*, Judd thought, but he still wasn't sure.

When the men walked up the path, Judd gasped. Some weird kind of weapon was slung over their shoulders. One was an older man with a beard and a dark hat. The other was younger and walked faster, as if he were trying to beat the older man. He also wore a baseball cap pulled low to his eyebrows. Judd couldn't see details, but he was sure they weren't Tom and Luke.

Judd looked at Lionel with wide eyes and put a finger to his lips. Lionel looked pained, like something terrible was wrong. When he grabbed his throat, Judd figured it out.

Lionel's throat tickled and he wanted to reach for the water bottle, but the two men were right next to the fort. He closed his eyes and swallowed, but his throat was parched and it felt like he was swallowing dry leaves.

For the first time Lionel saw the men's faces. The older one had a long scar that disappeared beneath his thick beard. The younger man had long, blond hair and carried his weapon slung over his left shoulder. As he walked, his right arm flopped lazily at his side. Lionel looked closer. The man's arm stopped at the elbow. He had no forearm or hand.

"Todd says he has a good lead on some who were holed up out on the island," One

Arm said. "From the tracks and stuff they left behind, he thinks there might have been as many as twenty-five or thirty of them."

"Mmmm," Scarface growled.

"You know how many Nicks a group like that could bring us?"

"We have to catch them first."

Lionel noticed the prominent mark of Nicolae on the young man's forehead and the number of the United North American States on the older man's arm. These two didn't seem like GC workers, but whoever they were, Lionel didn't want to get caught by them.

His throat scratched again, and Lionel gritted his teeth, trying to hold back a cough. He pressed a thumb and forefinger to his windpipe as hard as he could, but it didn't help. Finally, he put a hand over his mouth and gasped, letting out a cough.

The two men stopped.

THIRTEEN

Bounty Hunters

JUDD sat still, his eyes riveted on the two men. They were maybe twenty yards away now. If Judd and Lionel took off into the trees, there was a chance they could get away, but the weapons the men carried worried him. They looked a little like high-tech shotguns, but the silver barrels were bigger.

Scarface pulled the weapon from his shoulder and clicked it. A high-pitched hum sounded as One Arm dipped his left shoulder and with one motion turned on his weapon and held it up.

"You heard it too?" One Arm said.

Scarface scanned the area, and Judd tried to stay perfectly still. "Sounded like a cough. Could be them." The two walked a few paces the other way.

Judd put a hand out and found a hand-sized rock. He waited until the men had gone a little farther into the woods and threw the rock as far as he could. The rock hit and bounced on the ground, sounding like someone was running away.

"Over there," Scarface yelled, and they ran toward the trees.

Judd and Lionel quietly picked up their backpacks and scampered toward the path, shoulders stooped, heads low. The men thrashed about in the underbrush, but Judd knew they had only seconds before the two stopped and listened for movement.

Judd made it back onto the trail and quickened his pace. Lionel moved in behind him, wheezing and trying to hold back his coughs. Judd stopped as they went over a rise and ducked below the path. The men walked back into the open.

Judd ducked. "I hope they don't come this way."

Lionel closed his eyes and tried to stifle another cough. Judd grabbed a water bottle from his backpack and handed it to him. Lionel took a gulp and nodded. "Thanks."

"We know you're here, Judah-ites!" One Arm said. "Come out and we won't hurt you."

"Change your setting to stun," Scarface said. "I want to take these two alive."

Judd glanced at Lionel. "How do they know there are two of us?"

Lionel shrugged.

"Wish we had the dogs," One Arm said. "You think we should get the GC involved?"

"Nah, we'll lose money," Scarface said. "Let's split up."

Judd waved Lionel to follow and they backtracked along the path, trying to stay out of sight of the men.

Vicki wished she could hop in a car and drive to South Carolina. By her calculations, Judd and Lionel should have already landed. She asked God to help them find Luke and Tom Gowin and debated whether to send an e-mail to the southern command of the Young Tribulation Force. Though she didn't want to appear anxious, she decided to send it.

Cheryl Tifanne had gained weight with her pregnancy, and the girl sought Vicki out. She told Vicki that Marshall Jameson was a trained paramedic and would help deliver her child. Becky estimated that Cheryl was about six months away from giving birth.

"I have to tell you this whole thing scares me a lot," Cheryl said. "I don't look forward to the pain."

"I remember when my mom had my little sister," Vicki said. "She let me be with her in the birthing room at the hospital."

"What was it like?"

"It was great. They made me go out right toward the end when things got intense, then brought me back in just after Jeanni was born."

Cheryl took Vicki's hand. "I want you to be there. You'd be really good at getting me through the tough part."

"I wouldn't miss it."

The computer beeped, and Vicki opened a message from Carl Meninger, the young man who had escaped to South Carolina after working inside the GC in Florida.

Tom and Luke went to pick up Judd and Lionel but haven't returned, Carl wrote. *Chang confirmed that the pilot let them off, but we haven't heard anything else. We had radio contact with Tom and Luke about an hour ago and asked if they had met Judd and Lionel, but the radio went dead. Please get everyone to pray.*

Vicki gathered the others, told them what she knew, and Zeke suggested they break into smaller groups. Vicki found it hard to concentrate. She kept waiting for the phone to ring or the computer to ding with an e-mail saying Judd and Lionel were okay, but she heard nothing.

Judd ran for his life, something he had grown
accustomed to during the past three years. He
still didn't know what the two men wanted,
but he wasn't going to stay and find out.

Judd kept a steady pace along the path,
trying not to go so fast that he wouldn't have
energy for a burst of speed if he needed it.
Lionel was in good shape and kept up,
though his breathing had become labored.

They no longer heard or saw the men, and
Judd was glad. They darted away from the
path and neared a dirt road. Lionel jabbed
Judd's shoulder and pointed to his right.
"You think that belongs to them?"

A dusty, red pickup truck with a camper on
the back tilted in a ditch. Judd started the
other way, then heard banging. "Is that
coming from the truck?"

"Has to be," Lionel said.

They scurried toward the truck, and the
banging grew louder. Judd kept an eye on the
side mirrors and glanced in the back. When
he was sure there was no one in the cab, he
edged closer to the camper and rubbed the
dusty window. Three bodies lay on the truck
bed. One of them was kicking at the window,
but the others were still.

Lionel watched for the men as Judd tried to unlatch the camper. It was locked. Judd saw plastic handcuffs on the struggling man. He had a gag in his mouth and was frantically trying to speak. The man had the mark of the believer.

Judd held up a hand and whispered, "Hang in there. We'll get you out."

Judd knew if he smashed the camper's window the men would hear. He tried to lift the camper but it was secured, and the other windows were locked.

Lionel found the passenger door unlocked, climbed inside, and motioned to Judd. Inside, they found no access to the camper, and Judd started to sweat. "We've got to get out of here, but there's no way we can leave that guy."

"Do you know how to hot-wire a truck?" Lionel said.

"No, you?"

Lionel shook his head and rifled through the glove compartment while Judd looked under the seats for a spare key. The floor was messy, strewn with fast-food wrappers and coffee-stained Styrofoam cups. The small backseat was covered with shirts, pants, and a pair of wading boots. A black box held several square cartridges, and Judd figured they were ammunition for the weapons the men carried.

"Take a couple of these and throw the rest in the woods," Judd told Lionel as he searched the backseat. Judd hoped he would find another gun like the two were carrying but didn't. Instead, he discovered a toolbox, opened it, and found a long, flat-head screwdriver.

Judd grabbed it and raced to the camper, wedging the end of the screwdriver inside the lock and turning it back and forth. Nothing. He shoved the tool underneath the rear window and pushed with all his might. The gagged man followed Judd with his eyes. The glass squeaked but moved only a few inches. Suddenly, Judd saw a boot coming toward the window, and then shattered glass flew everywhere. The man inside scooted closer, and Judd removed his gag.

"I'm Tom Gowin! Get me out of here!"

"Those guys had to have heard that," Lionel said as they struggled to pull Tom out of the camper.

Judd nodded toward the bodies beside Tom. "Who are they?"

"Couple of undecided living on a marsh up the Colleton River. They're dead."

Judd felt for a pulse and realized Tom was

right. Just as Tom placed both feet on the road, Judd heard footsteps and the heavy breathing of the men in the woods.

"That way," Tom said, tilting his head, and the three rushed off in the other direction, away from the men, the road, and the truck.

"We should have flattened their tires," Lionel said. "Who are those guys, anyway?"

"Bounty hunters," Tom said.

They stopped talking as they hurtled through the bramble and trees.

One Arm yelled, "One of them got away! And they've wrecked the camper!"

Judd didn't look back, didn't want to think about the men chasing them with the strange weapons. He kept going as the wind picked up and blew tree limbs in front of them. Tom was running with his hands behind his back, so Judd placed a hand on one arm and Lionel took the other to help steady him.

The three were able to move quickly through the flat countryside and get a lead on the men. They had run for a good half hour when Tom signaled them to duck behind a huge tree with Spanish moss hanging from its branches. They sat, trying to catch their breath, listening for the men.

"Where's your brother Luke?" Lionel whispered.

"Luke got away," Tom said.

"What happened?" Judd said.

Tom tried to get in a comfortable position, but the handcuffs were cutting off his blood flow. He had to lie on his side to relieve the pain. "We were coming to meet you. Parked our minivan a few miles from the fort. We made sure no one followed us, but all of a sudden we heard a car pull up. Luke and I split up, which we probably shouldn't have done. The two guys spotted me. I would have lost them if I hadn't tripped and smashed my leg."

Judd looked at Tom's right leg. He hadn't noticed, but blood was caked on his pant leg. He pulled the clothing up, and Tom stifled a cry. The skin was torn from Tom's leg almost to the bone. Judd couldn't believe Tom could walk with that kind of a wound, let alone run for the past half hour.

"Did they shoot you with those guns?" Lionel said.

"Didn't have to. And if they had, I'd probably be dead like those other guys."

"How do you know they're bounty hunters?"

"I heard them talking about how much they were going to make off the three of us."

"You mean the GC is paying for dead believers?" Lionel said.

"Not just believers, anybody without the mark."

"Wait," Judd said, "Chang said the code name for the new program in the States was BoHu."

"Bounty hunters," Lionel said.

They sat in silence for a moment, resting.

"Do you know anything about those guns?" Judd said.

"I've never seen them before, but I know they have different settings for kill or stun."

"Do they shoot bullets?" Judd said.

"I think it's an energy beam or a laser."

"We heard them say something about searching for people on an island and that they weren't there anymore," Lionel said.

Tom frowned. "So they know about that. We had a really good hiding place, but one of the new members got careless and led someone to us. We've moved to an old plantation house that was standing during the Civil War."

"How do you keep GC away?" Judd said.

"We put up signs that say the place is condemned and that there are hazardous materials stored around the property. So far the GC has believed it, and they've left us alone."

"Can you take us back there?" Lionel said.

"It's going to be a hike, but I'll try. I had

hoped Luke would come back for me, but something must have happened to him."

Judd felt the air coming easier now and helped lift Tom out of the hiding place. "They seemed to know about Lionel and me. How?"

"They took my radio," Tom said. "Carl's back at the hiding place and must have said something."

"Point us in the right direction and we'll help you run," Judd said.

Tom got his bearings and nodded to the left. They set out at a fast clip, watching for any sign of the two men.

Tom stopped. Judd was about to ask why when he heard it—the sound that anyone on the run hated.

Dogs.

FOURTEEN

The Chase

JUDD recalled the guard dogs that had chased him at the Stahley home near Chicago. These dogs wailed as they followed the trail.

"They've got my scent," Tom said. "You guys take off, and I'll stall them."

"No way," Lionel said. "We're together now."

Judd agreed and the three continued.

"We'll never hide from those dogs," Tom said. "We need to find a ride. There's a bigger road in that direction."

"Let's go," Judd said.

They tromped through a marshy area and up an incline. Their feet were wet, and they were getting hot. Judd ran into a massive spider's web and fell back, flailing his arms at the sticky strands. The spider wasn't in sight, but Judd knew it had to be huge.

The barking snapped Judd back to reality.

A spider bite wouldn't matter if those men caught him. He pulled himself up the incline and grabbed Tom's arm as they reached a knoll. Turning, Judd saw movement below.

"That way," Tom said as he ran a few steps to the east. The ground was level again. Deerflies buzzed about their heads, circling for the kill. Tom asked Judd to swat at some on the back of his neck, and Judd tried to keep them away.

"Between the mosquitoes and the flies, there's not going to be much left of us when those guys catch us," Lionel said.

Judd knew there were ticks and chiggers in the back country, but he was set on one thing: escape. A few hours ago he had been in the safety of Petra, and before that, the beautiful garden at the chateau in France.

Vicki's face flashed in his mind.

"Please, God," Judd prayed, "help us get out of this."

Lionel swatted at mosquitoes whining around his head and pushed farther. The low hum of tires on pavement came from just ahead. "We're close," he whispered as they trampled through the brittle pine needles and towering palmettos.

The dogs were close when Lionel shoved through some tall grass and into the open near the road. A vehicle traveling from the south was heading toward them, but the sunlight blinded Lionel.

"Be careful!" Tom said, but Lionel had already committed. He waved his hands, hoping it was Luke coming back to help them.

As the vehicle neared, Lionel felt a pain in his chest. It was a truck. Red. Camper on the back. A radio crackled inside. "Do you see them yet?" a tinny voice said.

Scarface pulled closer as Lionel turned and ran into the woods, toward the dogs. "Yeah, I got 'em."

After breakfast with the others, Vicki went to her cabin. She had been inspired by Sam Goldberg's writings to write in her diary again. She hoped someday to show her words to Judd.

Each morning since coming to the new safe house she had pulled out a notebook she found in the supply building and wrote down her thoughts and feelings. At times she would write out a verse that struck her. Other times she wrote prayers. She already had pages of material.

She liked writing out the words. She had taken a typing class and was pretty fast, but there was something she enjoyed about moving her hand along the page with a pen, deciding on the right word, thinking through her feelings.

I don't want to get too excited about Judd's return, she wrote. *Part of me wants to jump out of my skin. I'd like to hop in Marshall's car and drive to South Carolina right now. But I've waited so long that a few more days won't hurt.*

Vicki had been praying for Judd, not just that he would come back and like her, but that he would become the person God wanted him to be.

She had written part of a prayer that Paul had prayed for the believers in Ephesus and changed it a little to make it more personal. *God, I ask you to give Judd spiritual wisdom and understanding, so he might grow in the knowledge of you. I pray that his heart will be flooded with light so he will understand the wonderful future you have promised all who believe in Jesus. Help Judd understand the incredible greatness of your power to do mighty things through him.*

Vicki added, *And, Lord, I ask that you bring Judd here quickly and change me too. Show us clearly whether we're supposed to be just friends or more than that.*

As she wrote, Vicki felt like she was not just writing to some ambassador in the sky or heavenly being who checked off a list of requests, but that she was actually talking to a real person who cared. There had been times when she had prayed out loud or silently that she felt God was distant and hadn't heard a word she had said. But writing out her prayer where she could see it somehow made a difference.

And please let Judd and Lionel have a good time with Luke, Tom, Carl, and the other believers in South Carolina.

Judd had moved closer to the road when the truck taillights flashed red and he recognized the vehicle as the camper. The dogs barked louder, running up the incline behind Judd and Tom.

"Go back!" Lionel shouted. "It's them!"

Lionel bounded into the brush as Judd and Tom raced away. Judd thought of throwing his backpack down to throw the dogs off, but he didn't want anyone finding their computer. There simply wasn't time to do anything but run.

The truck door slammed, and Judd heard voices on the radio. *How many are after us?* he thought. *They must have called in backup. Is it the GC?*

Lionel caught up to them and helped pull Tom along. They were running parallel with the road when an engine revved and Judd noticed the truck rolling backward beside them. "We need to go further in!"

"The dogs will get us," Lionel yelled.

The truck screeched to a halt, and a door flew open. Judd kept his head down, running as close to the ground as he could. He sensed someone running along the road and tried to cut to his right, but the foliage was too thick.

Judd heard a click and Tom screamed, "Get down!"

The three hit the ground as a weird sound pierced the air above them. A tree limb above Judd trembled and crackled, and then the weird sound stopped.

"I think I got 'em," someone said from the road.

"You better have that thing on stun," another man said. "You know what they'll do if you shoot someone with Carpathia's mark?"

Click. "I got it on stun," the first man said.

Judd helped Tom up and the three raced ahead. Shouts from behind. Dogs closer. Judd could almost feel their breath. He glanced back as Scarface burst through the

underbrush and aimed his weapon. Judd
leaped in the air and pushed Lionel and Tom
to the ground.

The beam burst from the gun with a sizzle
and instantly hit Judd's skin. He felt a shock
through his whole body and crumpled to the
ground.

Lionel dropped with Tom and turned as Judd
screamed. Judd fell forward in a clump of
pine needles and lay motionless. Lionel
raised his hands and yelled, "Don't shoot!"

Tom knelt beside Judd while Lionel exam-
ined his friend. "If they had the weapon on
stun, he's probably just knocked out."

Scarface walked to Lionel and nudged him
backward with his weapon. The man stared
at Lionel's forehead. "Let me see your right
hand."

"I don't have the mark," Lionel said.

"On the ground, hands behind your back."
He pushed Tom with his foot, and Tom fell
backward with an *oomph*. The dogs had
reached them and barked with abandon,
circling the three, sniffing and baying.
Scarface removed Lionel's backpack and
threw it on the ground, then pulled out
another set of plastic handcuffs and zipped

them onto Lionel's hands. They were too tight, but Lionel was afraid to say anything.

Another man Lionel hadn't seen before ran up, panting and sweating. He patted the dogs and inspected the prisoners. "I get a piece of this action?" Dog Man said.

"I stopped them before the dogs ever got here," Scarface said.

"Now hold on. I chased them toward you just like you asked. If I'd have known you wouldn't give me a cut—"

"Stop your bellyachin'. I'll give you half of one of them."

The man looked at the ground, then squinted at Scarface. "That's less than 20 percent! You know, this is going to seriously hurt our relationship—"

"Stop."

"I mean it. I got dogs to feed. You cut me out like this and next time you call I might not show up."

Scarface pulled Lionel to his feet and waved a hand. "All right, you can have this one."

Lionel kept an eye on Judd and didn't say anything. At some point he had to run, but with the third man approaching from the road, this clearly wasn't the time.

"I don't want to take him to the GC," Dog Man said. "I don't trust those people."

"Then I'll have to charge a small handling fee."

"Fine, half of one of these. Just bring me the money."

The man collared the dogs and walked away. Judd remained unmoving on the ground. Lionel wished he had checked Judd's pulse. Maybe Judd was playing possum and planned to jump the men.

Scarface patted Lionel's pockets and found his pocketknife and clips for the man's weapon. "So this is where they went." He shoved the cartridges in his pocket.

One Arm finally made it and helped Scarface cuff Judd.

"Is he okay?" Lionel said.

"What does it matter?" One Arm said. "I guess the GC could be soft on a couple of ratty-looking kids and let you take the mark, but most of the time they just chop away." He grinned and chuckled as he led Lionel back to the truck and placed him beside the dead bodies.

Lionel closed his eyes, took a deep breath, and coughed. He had never been this close to the dead before, and the smell made him queasy. The bounty hunters returned with Judd and Tom a few minutes later, placed them by Lionel, and closed the tailgate.

"Wait," Tom said. "I can tell you where to find more people without the mark."

Scarface had walked around the corner of the truck. He stuck his head through the cracked window. "I'm listening."

"Let my friends go and I'll tell you where you can find a hundred people like us."

"A hundred?" One Arm said.

"I'll even take you there," Tom said.

Scarface rolled his eyes. "Right. We let them go, and then you clam up." He leaned on the back of the truck and cocked his head. "I'll make you a deal. You lead us to a hundred other people and I'll let all three of you go, assuming your friend there lives. Sometimes the stun setting at close range does more damage."

"Deal," Tom said. "Could you get us something to eat, though? We're starving."

"Yeah, room service coming right up," the man sneered. "First thing is get those stiffs to the authorities."

The two men climbed in front and drove away. Lionel strained to hear their conversation but couldn't over the road noise. With his back to Judd, Lionel scooted near enough to his friend's hands and felt for a pulse. He found a faint throb, and a wave of relief swept over him.

"Are you really going to tell them where

they can find other people without the mark?" Lionel said to Tom.

"I'd never take them to other believers, but if we can give Luke more time to find us, maybe he can get us out."

The truck bounced along rutted back roads. Lionel prayed for a miracle but agreed with Tom. No matter what these bounty hunters did, they couldn't give up the others.

FIFTEEN

Bounty Hunters' Lair

JUDD awoke on a wood floor watching a ceiling fan turn above him. His head ached like it had been sawed in two and stitched together with a toothpick. His arms and shoulders throbbed, and his throat was parched. He rolled onto his side and tried to flex his hands to get the blood flowing again. He had no idea how he had gotten into this dusty room. Old wicker furniture sat stacked in a corner, and the windows had been covered with black plastic except for one behind the furniture. There was an "old socks" smell to the room that made Judd gag.

"He's waking up," someone said behind Judd. It was Tom Gowin. Tom and Lionel scooted closer and asked how he was feeling.

"Did I get run over by a truck? That's what it feels like."

Lionel explained what had happened and where they were. "Scarface took the truck and left One Arm. We still haven't eaten, and there's no word from Luke."

The door opened quickly, and One Arm stuck his head in, his long, blond hair swinging into the room after him. He looked at Judd and frowned. "You didn't die. You eat first. Get up."

Judd managed to get to his knees. The man grabbed him, and Judd yelped as his arm nearly popped out of the socket. One Arm kept an eye on Lionel and Tom, pointing Judd into the next room.

"Why can't we all eat?" Tom said.

"Max said one at a time, so shut up or you get nothing. I don't know why we're wasting food on you anyway."

As Judd walked through the door, the man shoved him with his stump and Judd lost his balance and fell, banging his head against the wooden floor.

The man slammed the door. "Poor baby. Now sit down or you're going back into your pen."

Judd sat, his head still spinning and his arms numb. One Arm slapped a paper plate in front of him with some chips and a sandwich.

"How am I supposed to eat with my hands behind me?"

"Animal style. Just dig in. What you don't finish I'll give to the other two."

Judd leaned down and picked up a potato chip with his teeth and crunched it. He wasn't hungry, but he knew he had to at least pretend to eat in order to stay.

"What's your name?" Judd said.

One Arm looked at him. "What do you care?"

"If my friends and I are about to make you rich, I ought to at least know your name."

The man smiled and Judd tried for another chip.

"You really gonna make me rich?"

"There's enough people hiding around here without the mark to keep you guys in business for years." When the man took a swig from a dusty beer can, Judd said, "How does it work, anyway? Do you take people to the GC and they hand you Nicks?"

One Arm frowned and shook his head. "Paperwork, paperwork. They tag the body, make sure they're not some kind of robot or dummy—which you could tell by lookin'. Then you show your ID and tag number, and they pay you through the mail. Max and I have caught about a dozen so far."

"How much per head?"

The man grinned. "Enough to make us want to keep catching them." He sat back and belched. "I don't know. I'd prob'ly help the GC catch these people for nothin' if they asked. Scumbags."

"But you won't turn down the money."

"Naw. We got ourselves a small business venture." One Arm took another drink. "Albert."

"Excuse me?"

"That's my name, Albert."

Judd scooted closer to the table. "Thanks. You know, you start feeling less than human when you get shot with—whatever that weapon is. I don't blame you—we are criminals for not taking the mark."

"Why didn't you take it? Just a little tattoo."

Since Albert had the mark of Carpathia, Judd assumed the man's destiny was sealed, but he had to be sure. "Did you worship the statue after getting the mark?"

"Of course. Say a few words, kneel, and go on. It's not that big a deal."

"Well, I just couldn't do it. I understand why you did, but . . ."

"You really are a Judah-ite then?"

Judd swallowed the potato chip he was

chewing and nodded. "I guess I'm toast with the GC."

Albert frowned. "Can't say they didn't warn you."

There was an awkward silence until Judd said, "You mind me asking what happened to your arm?"

Albert held out his stump and scratched the end. The skin had folded over where the elbow joint had been. "Curious-lookin' thing, ain't it?"

"I saw you handle that weapon with your left. You're pretty good."

"I'm left-handed naturally, so it wasn't that hard to get used to." He took the last swig of beer. "I was down in Florida, taking some time off. That was before I met Max. I decided to take a little swim one evening. Later they showed me the warning signs by the creek, but I didn't see them at the time."

"What happened?"

"Gator got me. He must have been watching me the whole time, lickin' his chops. Came up behind me, grabbed my arm, and tried to drag me under."

"You fought him?"

"You bet. I punched him in the eyes and did everything I could think of. I thought he had me when he rolled, flipped his body over. That's when I felt the crack. His teeth went through my arm, and he took the lower part of it with him."

"Did they catch him?"

Albert shook his head. "Somewhere there's a gator with half my arm in his stomach. Got my watch too."

The more Albert talked, the better Judd felt about their chances of getting away. If he could become friends, perhaps the man would have mercy on him and see him as a real person. "Did you lose a lot of blood?"

"Bled like a stuck pig. Somebody drove me to the hospital, and the doctors kinda fixed me up." He looked down at the stump again. "It's not pretty, but it's better than that thing dragging me to the bottom."

Judd took a small bite of the sandwich, and Albert leaned forward. "What'd it feel like gettin' shot with Max's new gun?"

Judd closed his eyes. "Felt like he dropped a truckload of electric eels on me."

Albert chuckled. "Imagine what those two in the truck felt like."

"Does it bother you at all, you know, killing people or taking them to the GC to be killed?"

Albert grew surly. "Why should it bother me? The GC says we're heroes, helping keep the peace. We're doing a favor to mankind."

Judd swallowed the stale bread. "Did anybody you know disappear?"

Albert stared at Judd and squinted. "Dinnertime's up." He pushed Judd out of the chair and toward the holding room.

"I didn't mean to upset you—"

"Just get inside and shut up."

Lionel was the last to eat. He tried the same approach as Judd, but nothing seemed to work with Albert. The man had opened another beer and turned on the television.

"What are we going to do when Max gets back?" Judd said.

"We have to get out of these handcuffs," Tom said. "Look around for something to cut them with."

"Even if we had two free hands, I don't think we'd be able to cut them off," Judd said.

"Maybe when he takes us out to look for people without the mark we can jump them," Lionel said.

"How?" Judd said. "They'll just push us to the ground and shoot us with that ray gun. And believe me, you don't want that."

"I think it's time to pray," Tom said.

Judd nodded, and the three of them bowed their heads. "God, I've never been in a situation as bad as this, but right now we want to trust in you. You delivered us from evil at Z-Van's concert, you saved us during the earthquake, and you've helped us each time we've been in trouble. Right now, we don't know what to do, so we're asking for wisdom. If this is the end, then we'll gladly come into your kingdom. But if you have more for us to do, please save us."

"I pray for Luke and the others, Lord," Lionel said, "that you would protect them through this. Keep them safe and help them spread the message of the death and resurrection of your Son."

Tom took a deep breath. "You've taught me a lot over the past couple of years, Lord. And I know there will be justice, because you work out your plan for your glory. So no matter what happens to us, we want you to be glorified. If you can be glorified most in our deaths, then let that be. But if we can help tell others about you and maybe keep some people safe by escaping, then let that happen. We commit ourselves into your hands."

They softly prayed the Lord's Prayer. Lionel noticed Judd's voice cracked when he came to the words, "but deliver us from the evil one."

At the end of the prayer, Tom began Psalm 23. Lionel had heard his mother recite the psalm since he was a boy, and he had read it at funerals his entire life, but he hadn't appreciated the words until now. Lionel felt his chin tremble as they whispered the words. "'Even when I walk through the dark valley of death, I will not be afraid, for you are close beside me. Your rod and your staff protect and comfort me.'"

Lionel let Judd and Tom finish the prayer. All three had wet eyes at the last verse: "'Surely your goodness and unfailing love will pursue me all the days of my life, and I will live in the house of the Lord forever.'"

Vicki couldn't wait any longer. She took Marshall's secure phone and walked into an empty cabin. Her fingers shook as she dialed Judd. It rang several times, but there was no answer. She waited a few minutes, then tried again. On the third ring someone with a gruff voice answered.

"Judd?"

"No, he's not here, but I can give him a message."

There was noise in the background, like the man was driving. "Who is this?"

The man ignored the question. "Why don't you tell me where you are and I'll make sure Judd finds you."

Vicki's stomach churned. Something wasn't right. Had Judd fallen into GC hands? She tried to still her shaking voice. "If you do anything to him, I'll—"

"You'll what?" The man laughed. "Come here and rescue your little Judah-ite friend? Well, bring it on, miss. I could use a few more just like you."

The phone clicked and Vicki felt sick. How did he get Judd's phone? And how did he know Judd was a follower of Tsion Ben-Judah?

When she approached the main cabin, there was activity inside.

"Vicki, we've been looking for you," Shelly said. "We just got an urgent message from New Babylon."

Vicki raced to the monitor. Mark stepped aside and let her read the message.

To: Judd and the rest of the Young
     Tribulation Force
Fr: Your friend
Re: New GC program

You won't be seeing this on the news, but I discovered what Commander Fulcire has begun. It's a pilot program that will spread throughout the world if successful. Fulcire has hired some lowlifes throughout the country to become bounty hunters. These are people looking for anyone without the mark of Carpathia. Doesn't matter if they bring them in dead or alive, they still get paid a bundle of Nicks.

The GC hopes this will work in the States. If it does and the bounty hunters don't kill marked citizens by mistake, the GC will expand the program in the next few months to let anyone arrest or kill an unmarked citizen.

This means we need to work hard to protect every believer not in Petra. I've sent this message throughout the network of believers, but please pass the word. And if you meet anyone without the mark, tell them to make their decision for God now.

Vicki sat back in the chair and moaned. She told the others about the phone call.

Mark immediately grabbed the phone and dialed Tom and Luke in South Carolina. "We have to warn them before they walk into a trap," he said.

Vicki shook her head. "I think that's exactly what they've done."

Judd heard the truck pull up to the shack with its squeaky brakes. The door slammed, and Albert whooped in the next room. "You got the money already?"

Something banged on the table. "They paid us for the others from last week, and I cashed the check. Your half is in there along with some supplies."

"Carpathia be praised!" Albert sang. "Look at all this. And think how much we'll get if those kids in there tell us where to find a hundred more!"

Max grumbled and a chair scraped the floor. "How'd it go here?"

"I let them eat just like you said. They didn't try anything, though one of them got a little mouthy."

Footsteps. The door opened. Max leaned in and smiled. "Which one of you is Judd?"

Judd lifted his chin. "Me."

"Some young lady called you. Sounded upset. You got a girlfriend?"

Judd clenched his teeth.

Max entered and knelt in front of Judd. "I could send her a lock of your hair. Or better yet, I'll put your head in a basket and airmail it to her."

Albert came to the door and stood beside Max. "We find her, and we can put 'em both in the same basket. You know the old saying, two heads are better than one."

The men laughed. Max glanced at Tom.

"These two talk funny. They're obviously not from here, so we're going to get rid of them. If you can lead us to this nest you were talking about, it might save your life."

Tom started to protest, but Max put a foot in his chest and kicked hard. Tom flew back, his head cracking the floor. The two men seized Judd and Lionel and pulled them to their feet.

"Where are you taking us?" Judd said.

"You've got a little appointment with the GC," Max said. "I told them about you and they want to see you."

"Yeah," Albert sneered. "Time for you two to feel the blade."

ABOUT THE AUTHORS

Jerry B. Jenkins (www.jerryjenkins.com) is the writer of the Left Behind series. He owns the Jerry B. Jenkins Christian Writers Guild, an organization dedicated to mentoring aspiring authors. Former vice president for publishing for the Moody Bible Institute of Chicago, he also served many years as editor of *Moody* magazine and is now Moody's writer-at-large.

His writing has appeared in publications as varied as *Reader's Digest, Parade, Guideposts,* in-flight magazines, and dozens of other periodicals. Jenkins's biographies include books with Billy Graham, Hank Aaron, Bill Gaither, Luis Palau, Walter Payton, Orel Hershiser, and Nolan Ryan, among many others. His books appear regularly on the *New York Times, USA Today, Wall Street Journal,* and *Publishers Weekly* bestseller lists.

Jerry is also the writer of the nationally syndicated sports story comic strip *Gil Thorp,* distributed to newspapers across the United States by Tribune Media Services.

Jerry and his wife, Dianna, live in Colorado and have three grown sons.

Dr. Tim LaHaye (www.timlahaye.com), who conceived the idea of fictionalizing an account of the Rapture and the Tribulation, is a noted author, minister, and nationally recognized speaker on Bible prophecy. He is the founder of both Tim LaHaye Ministries and The PreTrib Research Center. He also recently cofounded the Tim LaHaye School of Prophecy at Liberty University. Presently Dr. LaHaye speaks at many of the major Bible prophecy conferences in the U.S. and Canada, where his current prophecy books are very popular.

Dr. LaHaye holds a doctor of ministry degree from Western Theological Seminary and a doctor of literature degree from Liberty University. For twenty-five years he pastored one of the nation's outstanding churches in San Diego, which grew to three locations. It was during that time that he founded two accredited Christian high schools, a Christian school system of ten schools, and Christian Heritage College.

Dr. LaHaye has written over forty books that have been published in more than thirty languages. He has written books on a wide variety of subjects, such as family life, temperaments, and Bible prophecy. His current fiction works, the Left Behind series, written with Jerry B. Jenkins, continue to appear on the best-seller lists of the Christian Booksellers Association, *Publishers Weekly*, *Wall Street Journal*, *USA Today*, and the *New York Times*.

He is the father of four grown children and grand-father of nine. Snow skiing, waterskiing, motorcycling, golfing, vacationing with family, and jogging are among his leisure activities.

The Future Is Clear

Check out the exciting Left Behind: The Kids series

Books #35 and #36 coming soon!

Discover the latest about the Left Behind series and complete line of products at

www.leftbehind.com

Hooked on the exciting
Left Behind: The Kids series?
Then you'll love the dramatic audios!

Listen as the characters come to life in this theatrical
audio that makes the saga of those left behind
even more exciting.

High-tech sound effects, original music,
and professional actors will have you
on the edge of your seat.

Experience the heart-stopping action and suspense of the end times for yourself!

Three exciting volumes available on CD or cassette.